I0588544

DAILY GRIND

and Other Astounding Stories of Mundane Matters

Chuck McKenzie

www.daftnotions.com

First published by Daft Notions in 2024
Daft Notions www.daftnotions.com
Melbourne, Victoria, Australia
Copyright © Chuck McKenzie

All rights reserved. No part of this book may be reproduced or transmitted in any form or by any means, including Internet search engines and retailers, electronic or mechanical, photocopying (except under the provisions of the Australian Copyright Act 1968), recording or by any information storage and retrieval system, without prior permission by the publisher.

National Library of Australia Cataloguing-in-Publication data.
Daily Grind and Other Astounding Stories of Mundane Matters

ISBN: 978-0-6458945-6-1 (paperback)
ISBN: 978-0-6458945-7-8 (ebook)

Spelling in this collection is standard Australian

Cover Design, Interior Artwork & Editing © All In The Edit
www.allintheedit.com

Fiction, Science Fiction, Short Stories

For Sarah, who loves me right back.

Contents

Daily Grind

Bip! Bip!

At the sound of the horn, Sloom came rushing out of his home and jumped into Vorn's skitter. "Hey."

"'Morning."

Sloom buckled himself in as the skitter quacked into nilspace. "How's things? Good weekend?"

"Yeah, not bad," Vorn said. "Yours?"

"Meh. So, where are we working today?"

"Earth. Schedule's in the glove box."

Sloom pulled a face.

Vorn shot him a look. "What?"

Sloom shrugged as he rummaged for the schedule. "It's just— y'know. *Earth*. It's such a dreary little hole. Places like that make me wonder what I'm doing in this job."

Vorn shrugged. "Pays well."

"Yeah, well, not everything's about the pay, y'know?"

The skitter plopped out of nilspace and fell to Earth. Sloom checked the schedule, then grabbed the flensing kit as they clambered out and moved towards their target.

"So," Vorn said, "the job's really getting you down, huh?"

Sloom sighed. "It's just…not what I pictured myself doing at my age."

The cow looked up as the barn doors opened. "Moo?"

Sloom opened the kit. He and Vorm selected the appropriate tools.

"MOO!" the cow exclaimed as Sloom removed its eyeballs. "GURGLE!" it added as Vorn removed its tongue. Sloom drained the cow's blood into a pouch. The cow fell over. Sloom and Vorn went back to the skitter.

"I mean, I've got a degree in Bacteriological Mnemonics," Sloom griped. "But it was such a hard field to get into after I graduated that I had to take this job just to pay the rent. I thought it'd be a short-term thing, y'know?"

The skitter bounced up and shot eastwards, dropping onto the roof of a very nice two-storey rural homestead, with a white picket fence and everything. Sloom and Vorn clambered down the side of the building to an upper-storey window, which they peered into. A piercing scream issued from within. They casually climbed back up to the skitter.

"I know you said it's not all about the money," Vorn said as they took off again, "but this level of pay surely takes some of the sting out of not being able to work in your preferred field?"

The skitter shot northwards, tumbling into a suburban backyard garden. Vorn and Sloom activated their chameleonware to assume native form, donned the black suits and sunglasses packed carefully in the trunk of the skitter, and made their way to the back door of the house.

"Look, yes, the money's great. But that's part of the problem." Sloom knocked at the door. "If I entered the Bacteriological Mnemonics industry now, at ground level, my starting salary would be less than half what I'm making now. And it could take years for me to work my way up to—"

Sloom abruptly fell silent as the door opened. The human occupant of the house stared at them. "Who are you? What are you doing in my yard?"

"Mister Tepid?" Vorn enquired.

"Yes?"

"Mister *James August* Tepid?" Sloom pressed.

"Yes?"

"Born nineteen sixty-five?" Vorn continued. "Graduated Lucemore High in nineteen eighty-three? Got off with Enid Kapler behind the Trent Street bus-stop in nineteen eighty-two? Single, never married? Habitually eats Aldi off-brand Corn Flakes for breakfast? Suffers from piles? Prefers womens' underwear because it's—" Vorn gestured to indicate air quotes, "'More Comfortable'?"

"How the bloody hell—??"

"You spotted a UFO over your house last night, I believe?" Sloom cut in.

"Well…yes, but—"

Vorn nodded. "I see. Well. Don't tell anyone, Mister Tepid."

"Or else," Sloom added.

"Yeah. Or else," Vorn echoed.

"Got it?"

The door slammed shut. Vorn and Sloom returned to the skitter, where they changed back into something more comfortable. Moments later, the skitter bounded south.

"It wouldn't matter so much if I *enjoyed* this job," Sloom continued, as the skitter buzzed a lone hitchhiker wandering along the interstate. "Like I said, it's honestly not all about the money. Job satisfaction's important too, y'know? And I want to feel like I'm doing something *worthwhile*. But I'm *not* enjoying the job, I *don't* get any satisfaction from it, and I really don't feel like it's even slightly worthwhile!"

Vorn activated the suckybeam and drew the hitchhiker up into the skitter. "Oral or anal?"

"Do you know how dirty their mouths are?"

"Okay then."

"*Ooooooer!*" the hitchhiker squealed.

"At the end of the day," Sloom grumbled, "I want job satisfaction *and* wealth. And whether I stay or go, I'm going to sacrifice one or the other. All done?"

"All done. Give him the owl imprint and dump him."

The hitchhiker hit the ground, hooting maniacally.

Vorn glanced at his watch. "Clock-off time."

The flitter quacked into nilspace. Sloom began filling out shift paperwork.

"Look, here's an idea," Vorn offered. "Try to think of the job as something you *only* do for the money without expecting any satisfaction whatsoever, and apply for a low-paid Bacteriological Mnemonics *internship*. With your qualifications, you'd get in easy."

Sloom looked up from the paperwork. "An internship?"

"I mean, yeah, it's a lot of extra work, and badly paid, but you'll still have *this* job to pay the bills, and it shouldn't take you too long to adjust to the workload. Then you look at doing one or two nights a week for a few cycles, so it doesn't interfere with your day job, and pretty soon you'd have sufficient experience to walk straight into a high-level position with a great salary!"

Sloom nodded thoughtfully. "Huh. Wealth *and* satisfaction, but spread across two separate jobs."

"Exactly!"

"*And* I'd be doing something worthwhile, even as an intern!" Sloom gave Vorn a warm smile. "Thanks, mate. I really appreciate the advice. And the support. I'm gonna get on to this as soon as I get home tonight!"

Vorn punched Sloom's shoulder playfully. "That's the way. And hey, for what it's worth, I do get how you've been feeling about this job."

"Really? I thought you loved it."

"Oh, don't get me wrong, I *do* love it." Vorn glanced at Sloom's paperwork. "I mean, mutilation, intimidation, abduction, probing. For me, that's job satisfaction right there. But," he shrugged, "even I have days where I can't help but wonder…well, whether there's really any *point* to it all…"

Time Spent With A Cat

"You're about to get a visitor," said the cat, sitting on—or rather, hovering about a centimetre above—the edge of my desk. It glanced pointedly towards the wall behind my chair, where my framed certificate hung.

State of Victoria
Department of Law Enforcement
Private Investigators Licence
James Carpenter

"Might want to straighten that up," the cat continued. "You really can't afford to look sloppy in front of clients right now, can you?"

I hate cats. I really do. Feral, lazy, arrogant creatures. So it does seem unnecessarily ironic that my Conscience took the form of a talking calico cat. Maybe the current popular theory about Consciences being 'shared subconscious projections' is crap after all. Or maybe I just really do hate myself that much. Four whole months since everyone, worldwide, got a Conscience, and still nobody can explain a damned thing about it. All *I* knew for sure is that my previously thriving business had pretty much ground to a halt as society worked through the resulting chaos.

"Up yours," I snapped, and flicked the pen I'd been holding at the cat. The pen, of course, passed right through the animal and clattered against the floorboards.

There was a knock on the door. Three sharp raps.

I bit down on the follow-up insult I'd been about to hurl at the cat. I'd already learned the hard way that potential clients get twitchy if they catch you swearing at a cat, even a possibly imaginary talking cat that everyone can see and hear. I stood up, angrily buttoning my coat. "Come in," I called, forcing a smile

Of all the people I might have guessed would be at the door when it opened, Alan Cook wouldn't have been one of them. I felt an expression of shock touch my face momentarily before I was able to clamp down on it, staring impassively at my visitor.

Alan nodded, flashing a smile that vanished almost immediately. "Hey, Jim. Long time, no see."

I said nothing.

Alan shuffled uncomfortably for a moment, standing there in full military uniform with his cap tucked underneath his arm. "May I come in?"

I sat down again, carefully considering my response. Clearly taking my failure to scream abuse as an invitation, Alan stepped into my office, leaving the door open behind him, which only fuelled my irritation.

There was a long, awkward pause.

"Well," I said eventually. "This…is a surprise."

Alan gestured towards the empty chair facing my desk. "May I?"

I made a vague gesture. Alan took a seat, placed his cap on the desk in front of him, then glanced around at the bookshelves and filing cabinets lining the walls. I opened my mouth to speak again, and at that moment a tall figure walked in through the open door behind Alan. "Holy crap!" I said.

Alan's Conscience bowed, his eyes remaining locked with mine as he treated me to a huge grin that shone blindingly white against ebony skin. "*Beau*-ti-ful day, Sah! Allow me to introduce myself—"

"Baron Samedi," I interrupted. "From the movie 'Live and Let Die'." I gave Alan a look. "I never knew you were a James Bond fan."

Alan sighed. "I'm not. But we both know that counts for nothing." He glanced pointedly at the cat on my desk.

Samedi laughed delightedly and clapped his hands together. "Just so, Sah! Just so!" His voice was rich and creamy, exactly as I remembered it sounding in the film.

"Well, I'm starting to feel better about being stuck with an animal I despise," I said. "Better than being stuck with what probably comes across nowadays as an Uncle Tom routine."

Alan's normally pale face turned crimson. "It's no bloody joke, Jim! Half the people I interact with now assume I'm a dyed-in-the-wool racist!"

"You're not?"

The crimson tone deepened. "No, I'm bloody not!"

"Well, if it's any consolation, in 'Live and Let Die' Samedi used his seemingly subservient demeanour to cover the fact that he was actually a pretty damn scary dude. Powerful and deadly. Almost took out Roger Moore with a machete."

"Gee. Thanks so much for that. I'll send a memo around the office."

I smiled thinly. "Unlike you, I *am* a fan. Want to swap?"

"Hey!" the cat protested.

"I wish!" Alan began to relax into his chair. "Wouldn't *that* make life a whole lot—"

"Alan?" I interrupted.

"Yes?"

"What do you want?" I asked, wishing I hadn't thrown the pen at the cat, so I could tap it against the desk to indicate how valuable my time was.

Alan drummed the fingers of both hands against the desktop for a moment. He looked stressed, but that's what the army does to you. He was plumper than when I'd last seen him, with a colonel's insignia on his shoulder-board. His uniform was beautifully clean and laundered, which meant he was either in a relationship, or far better domesticated than when we'd been cadets together. It looked like staying with the army had been good for Alan. And that stung. I'd been the one who'd been expected to rise through the ranks, after all.

"I wanted to offer you a job," Alan said, at the same time as Samedi piped up, "He wants to apologise, Sah."

Alan turned sharply in his chair. "Will you please be quiet?"

"Well, which is it?" I asked, glancing back and forth between them.

"Both would be good," the cat said, and I felt an unfamiliar glow of camaraderie, which faded quickly.

Alan looked at the cat, then back at me. "It talks."

"It does," the cat confirmed. "Well spotted."

I resisted the urge to snap my fingers in Alan's face to get him to focus. "Well?" I pressed.

Alan visibly floundered for a moment, and I almost felt bad for him. Almost. "Yeah. Both," he admitted. "Look, Jim—I'm truly sorry."

I waited.

"I never asked you to take the rap for me," he went on, "but…"

"But?"

Alan shrugged. "I should have spoken up. I know that. They clearly knew it was one of us, but I guess neither of us thought *you'd* get booted out over it. And when you were, I should have 'fessed up. Apologised." There was an awkward pause. "I do understand if I'm just a bit too damn late with this, but…yeah. I'm sorry."

I opened my mouth, having no real idea of what I was about to say.

"Apology accepted," the cat said, before I could get a word out.

I turned to berate the cat, then realised that despite the emotions stirred up by Alan's visit the anger just…wasn't there anymore. "Yeah." I gave Alan a look, nodding slowly. "Sure. Okay. We're cool."

Alan did his best to maintain a military demeanour, but I saw how he sagged slightly in his chair. This clearly hadn't been easy for him. Not that I was ready to fully forgive him.

"So anyway, how the heck are you a colonel already?" the cat asked Alan. *A fair question,* I thought. It takes a minimum twenty-one years to go from officer cadet to colonel, even assuming one has the drive, ability and suitability for an army career. Last I'd seen Alan— just over fifteen years ago—he'd had none of the above, being an undisciplined party-brat looking for a blokey work culture to immerse himself in while he waited for his inheritance. The polar opposite of myself. Another reason why getting kicked out of the army had hurt me so badly.

Alan cleared his throat. "Look…what happened to you was a massive wake-up call for me. I knuckled down. Pushed myself. Had some lucky breaks along the way. And, if I'm honest, some rules were bent to get me to where I am now because it turned out I had a certain…*efficiency*…in overseeing tech projects."

"Special Operations, huh?"

Alan said nothing.

"I bet it's Special Weapons," the cat said, in a sing-song voice.

Alan gave the cat a sharp look.

"*Definitely* Special Weapons," the cat fake-whispered to me, extremely loudly.

Samedi inclined his head slightly. "We cannot tell you that, Sah. Unless, of course, you wish to take the job...?"

I drummed my fingers against the desktop for a moment. "Okay. So what's the job?"

"Homicide investigation."

"What? A murder?" I gave Alan an incredulous look. "Why the hell wouldn't the military police be dealing with that?"

Alan looked down at the desk, then back at me. "There are…complications," he admitted. "The deceased isn't military, and wasn't conducting her research on military grounds. She runs a private research company, and was about to pitch what she suggested would be a game-changing piece of tech to us. It could be…bad…on several levels if anyone directly connected to the military went barging in to investigate."

The cat tilted its head quizzically. "Why not the regular police, then?"

"Yeah, good question," I said. "Well?"

Alan cleared his throat again. "Well, the fact is that the tech in question, whatever it may be, was developed by the contractor using military funding, and if that information was leaked, even accidentally, by anyone outside of our department, it could have…repercussions."

I raised an eyebrow, and sensed the cat doing the same. "Repercussions?"

"Security repercussions. Such as hostile parties targeting the private companies we deal with."

"So, just to be clear, Special Weapons is funding research by offsite private companies—presumably not provided with military protection, by the sounds of it—as, what? Private contractors? Why wouldn't this be conducted at a military base, and by your own people?"

"It's a newish policy I implemented," Alan explained. "We take the budgeted research funds and, rather than allocating the full funding to our own developmental groups, we spread it across numerous private companies that are looking into areas we think may prove interesting, with the contractual stipulation that we get first pick of anything of value they come up with."

"So these companies receive a sort of retainer?"

"Exactly. The funds tend to encourage a greater commitment to the research these companies are undertaking—"

"So it's actually a bribe?" the cat interrupted.

"It's an *inducement*," Alan said firmly. "And because we're not funding the entire process for any given company, our budget goes further than if we kept it all in house. We can spread it across a greater number of specialist bodies, which yields greater results."

"And when these companies discover something amazing, you swoop in and grab it?" I asked.

"No," Alan said, looking rather aggrieved. "We don't just 'grab it.' We contractually agree to purchase the full rights to it, for a more than generous amount. After that, sometimes we provide additional funds for the company in question to further refine or produce the tech, and sometimes we take it off their hands and continue with further processes entirely in house, depending upon our requirements and circumstances. And the companies that come up with the goods tend to then receive ongoing funding to come up with more goodies. Everybody gets what they want."

"It all sounds frightfully civilised," I noted. "So, in a nutshell, you don't want outsiders trampling all over this murder investigation because you don't want them to mess with anything you've poured developmental money into?"

Alan nodded. "Exactly."

"Anything else I should know?"

Alan sighed. "Yeah. Well, we filed a motion in court to convince a judge that letting non-specialist investigators in on this was potentially dangerous to the public. Additionally, we reached a sort of compromise to ensure the investigation would be conducted by a non-military party so as to publicly distance ourselves from the case, with that party nominated by myself, while agreeing that I'd also personally remain in touch with the nominated investigator as a sort of safety liaison. You'd obviously have to submit full reports and sworn affidavits afterwards to disavow any possibility of collusion between you and I, but—"

"Okay, wait," I interrupted. Something just wasn't adding up here. "So, I get why you can't have the cops or the MPs involved. But in that case, why not approach someone with the precise specialist experience you need, like a scientist, or someone else from the company the victim worked for, or even just someone who knows their military tech? Because I'm guessing that whatever knowledge your investigator needs, I don't have it. Outside of the tools I use as a private investigator I don't have any major expertise in technology, let alone current military-grade tech, especially not after being out of the army for over a decade. Surely you could use the vast resources at your disposal to find and vet a suitable investigator, so I genuinely don't see why I'm your go-to guy for this investigation."

Alan exhaled loudly. "Because we don't have the *time* to find and vet an expert, whereas I knew I could immediately get the judge on board by citing *your* impressive record as a private investigator."

I nodded, not entirely surprised. Once you've been in the army, they never really stop watching you. And I figured maybe Alan had personally kept tabs on me for the same reason that some people like to check up on ex-partners: a creepy combination of nostalgia, guilt, and obsession. "Is the judge not aware of our…history?"

Alan clenched his jaw slightly. "Very much so. I came clean about everything. Full disclosure."

"That must have hurt," the cat said. I didn't have to look to know the animal was smiling smugly.

Alan nodded curtly. "Yes. But this is too important. I needed to demonstrate to the judge that you were one of the best at what you do, and that you weren't going to do me or the military any favours."

"Because Jim hates your guts," the cat stated helpfully.

"Hey, cool it!" I snapped at the cat.

Alan shrugged helplessly. "Okay, yeah. And also—"

I smiled thinly. "And also…because you could prove that that I can keep my mouth shut?"

"Just so," Samedi said gently. "Just so, Sah."

There was an awkward pause.

"Okay," I said eventually. "So why don't you have time to find the expert you *really* need, as opposed to a convenient ring-in?"

Alan fidgeted in his chair. "Well…the judge gave me a strict time limit on our nominee investigating the scene before she opens it up to the civilian police. She's just as concerned about the military contaminating evidence as she was about the cops screwing with hazardous tech. Police forensics are already on the scene, assisting us, but—"

"How long?" I interrupted impatiently.

"Six hours."

"FUCK!" the cat shouted. I bit down on a similar epithet, staring incredulously at Alan.

"From the time that I left the judge," Alan added. "Which was an hour ago."

I actually laughed. "Oh, okay then!"

Alan made a pleading gesture. "Look, I know it's ludicrous, but it's all I've been granted. So I need to know right now if you're in or out."

I hesitated.

"Look, we both know you don't owe me a damn thing," Alan continued, "but I'm over a goddamned barrel here, and the clock is ticking. If I can't solve this case to the judge's satisfaction within the allotted time, the law is going to swoop in and secure the crime scene themselves, with everything Scott was working on taken as evidence—computers, notes, materials, the lot—and it could take years for us to get it all back, assuming that we ever do, which is unacceptable. So how about we move right past talking this through and jump straight to me offering you a ludicrous amount of money to take on the investigation? You know, to compensate for the ludicrous situation?"

"How much money?" the cat asked.

"Samedi?" Alan prompted.

Samedi held up his right hand, palm facing towards me so I could see the dollar value that had materialised there, seemingly written in white chalk. *Interesting*, I thought. *Using his Conscience for secure communication.* "Your fee, Sah."

I blinked. My mouth may have dropped open slightly.

"Great poker face, dude," the cat muttered.

I mentally shook myself, regaining my composure. "Right. Okay. That seems…fine. And what if I don't actually solve the case?" I held up a hand as Alan opened his mouth. "To be clear, I will genuinely do everything humanly possible to crack this. But given the time limit—"

"I was going to say," Alan broke in, "that this is just your consultancy fee." The sum on Samedi's palm shifted and changed. "*That's* your final fee if you manage to close the case."

I actually swore this time.

The cat gave me a look. "That's a lot of kibble."

"Okay," I said. "Let's…I mean, I'm in."

Alan extended his hand across the desk. After a moment I stood, grasped it, and shook. "You can take me directly to the scene?"

"Car's waiting outside."

"Okay. Let's go."

"Look," Alan said, as we took the stairs three at a time down to the street, our Consciences floating beside us, "the time limit isn't necessarily as grim as it seems, because there's really no doubt about who committed the murder. I was already on premises with some of my team, awaiting a demo of the promised tech. We heard a brief, shouted argument, then a gunshot. Rushed in, saw the husband standing near the body, nobody else in the room, nobody else on premises, windowless room with a single point of access."

I frowned. "Sounds like an open-and-shut case. So what's the issue?"

It was Samedi who replied. "Because there's no weapon, Sah. No weapon at all."

Samedi wasn't wrong; there was no weapon whatsoever to be found. There was, however, a sizeable hole in Karen Scott's head, right where her left eye should have been.

"Forensic technicians have been sweeping the room from top to bottom." Alan gestured towards a young woman in sterile duds who was swabbing down a nearby workbench, accompanied by her Conscience, John Lennon. "This one's just giving it a once-over. Nobody's found much, other than chemical residues."

"Guess I won't bother with my own search, then. I assume someone's already checked the cameras to see what happened?"

Alan nodded towards the small dome cameras positioned on the ceiling in all four corners of the laboratory. "The cameras weren't on. Scott only ran them when she was actually working on whatever she was working on. I suppose she would have turned them on to record the pitch, but that doesn't help us now, obviously."

"No general security cameras?"

"Nope."

"Damn." I glanced at Scott's body again, then quickly looked away. As a private investigator I'd seen dead bodies before, despite dealing mostly with cheating spouses and internal corporate theft; however, most of those corpses had been nicely laid out on mortuary trays, prettied up for the purposes of identification. And I'd never seen a dead body during my time in the military, let alone been responsible for one, having never seen actual combat. The standard army process of completely breaking recruits down psychologically before rebuilding them as virtual automatons who wouldn't blink as they fired a gun at another human being hadn't progressed too far by the time I'd been unceremoniously ejected; thus, the sight of Scott lying spreadeagled where she'd collapsed—a chaotic jumble of limbs that unpleasantly contrasted the elegant navy business suit and skirt she was wearing, with that ragged hole in her head seeming to stare at me—shook me more than I'd expected. She appeared to be in her mid-to-late forties, and there was an expression of faint surprise frozen on her pallid face. No Conscience, of course; it would have vanished at the moment of death, which—if it turned out that Consciences *weren't* subconscious projections—seemed like pretty cruddy behaviour to me. No kids, Alan had told me. Just Scott and her husband, a lecturer at one of the second-tier Melbourne universities.

"Excuse me?" I called over to the technician. "Is there any chance we could…cover her up?"

The technician glanced at me, then nodded understandingly and started fishing some plastic sheeting out of the kit near her feet.

"What did that?" I asked Alan, gesturing towards the crater in Scott's face.

"They were checking when I left to see the judge. Hang on—" Alan addressed the technician as she came over—Lennon drifting along behind her—and knelt down to lay the sheeting over Scott's body. "Delgado, was it? Any word on the projectile?"

Delgado shrugged as she stood up again. "There, ah…doesn't appear to be one."

"It went straight through?" I looked down at Scott, now shrouded in plastic. Then I realised there'd been no blood pooling under her head.

"Nope," the technician said, confirming my thought. "We've been told we can't move her to the morgue just yet—" she shot a pointed look at Alan, "—so we performed a scan with a mobile x-ray unit. Whatever killed her drove itself well into her frontal cortex, but there's no projectile still in there, and no exit wound, and no sign that the projectile ricocheted straight back out of the entry wound. So," she shrugged, "I dunno. It's a weird one."

"Firearm?" I asked. "Or maybe something like a slingshot?"

"No, definitely a firearm," Delgado said. "There's powder burn across her eye socket and face. Shot at close range. But no bullet, or even fragments, which makes no sense whatsoever."

"Imaginary bullet from an imaginary gun," Lennon intoned. "Most peculiar, Mama."

The technician didn't respond, other than to give me a dark look. *This fucking guy*, the look said.

I nodded slightly, then glanced sideways to indicate the cat floating at my shoulder. *I feel your pain, lady.*

The corner of her mouth hooked upwards into a smile, almost. Then she nodded, and moved back to the bench.

I looked around the room. The building was one of those 1940s-style houses that had been converted to serve as both a workplace and a home, with a foyer at the front for receiving clients, and a private residence at the back. The room in which we now stood had been Scott's study-cum-workshop, separating the foyer from the home. A laminate desk and built-in bookcases full of textbooks dominated one side of the room; complex arrangements of glass tubing, pipettes, beakers and sinks spread across a couple of long, linoleum-covered benches on the other. Against the wall opposite the door, a metre-long aquarium full of small, colourful fish sat atop an enclosed wooden cabinet stand. Above this, a wall-mounted shelf held a mini stereo system with a few dozen CDs racked beside it, along with a mid-sized digital photo frame. On the work bench nearest us was a large, open-fronted plexiglass tank, the back wall of which was thickly coated in what appeared to be ballistics gel. Near the tank was a large serving tray upon which sat a number of fluted glasses, with a magnum of what I at first took to be sparkling wine, but then realised was genuine Moët & Chandon champagne, resting in an ice bucket in the middle.

I glanced at Alan. "So, you and your team rushed in here the moment you heard the shot. No time for the killer to properly dispose of the weapon?"

"I wouldn't have thought so. Couldn't have been more than twenty seconds between the shot and us bursting in here. Standard breaching procedure. Door was ajar, so we drew weapons and identified ourselves, husband yells out that he's unarmed, so we came in with weapons drawn, to find him standing there—" Alan indicated the spot, "—with his hands raised. Maybe thirty seconds at the outside."

"The husband did have powder residue on his hands, for what it's worth," Delgado piped up, turning to face us again. "But it's not enough evidence to convict him unless we can find the weapon, as it could have come from another source." She nodded at the plexiglass tank. "They were clearly working with ballistics, so…"

I nodded. "Okay. Cool, thanks." Delgado smiled, and she and her Conscience went back to their swabbing. I turned back to Alan. "Scott was doing ballistics testing in a room with an aquarium? That seems…potentially hazardous. Especially for the fish."

Alan shrugged. "Look, she actually didn't deal with ballistics, regardless of what Delgado said."

"So why the tank of ballistics gel?"

Alan shrugged again.

I rubbed my chin thoughtfully. "So. So, so, so…"

"You have an idea, Sah?" Samedi asked.

"Where are we at?" I asked, more to myself than to anyone else.

"Well," the cat said, "we know she spent a lot of time in here."

I opened my mouth to tell the cat to shut up, then hesitated. "Go on."

"Well, the room's set up for both admin *and* practical chemistry work, so she probably did almost all of her work in here. And the sound system and aquarium suggest that she spent enough of each working day in here to want to make the room more…homely. Look, she even has CDs."

I nodded slowly. CDs were personal belongings with sentimental value. Most people would just rely upon Spotify for workplace tunes.

The cat was right: this had been a living area almost as much as it was a workspace. It was obvious, really, and I'd certainly have noticed it myself eventually, regardless of the cat pipping me to the post in terms of collating that information into a concrete observation. *Interesting.* "So she was a workaholic."

"Which could have been putting a strain on her marriage. Or maybe she threw herself into work to escape an already crappy marriage." The cat gave a very human-looking shrug.

Good thinking. "Yeah. A chat with the husband is in order, I think." I glanced at the tray of champagne glasses. "She was clearly prepped for a congratulatory drink." I turned to Alan. "So…you and your team were already here when you heard the shot, yeah? In the foyer?"

"Yes, that's right."

"And had you seen her at all today before she was killed?"

"Yeah, briefly. She came out to say hello, let us know she wouldn't be long, that sort of thing. That was about five minutes before we heard the shot."

So Scott had definitely been alive just before this whole thing went down. "How did she seem?"

Alan thought about it. "Excited. Rushed, maybe a little stressed. But she did say she'd only just gotten back from a week away in Sydney, so she was probably trying to finalise prep for the demo."

"Huh," the cat said.

Alan and I both gave the animal a look. "What?" I asked.

"Well…just seems odd that a highly successful scientist would be running behind the eight ball to prepare a demonstration with so much financial success riding on it." The cat glanced at Alan. "Unless she was a bit lax that way?"

Alan looked at me. I raised an eyebrow.

"Well, no," Alan said. "She always seemed very professional. Meticulous."

"But obviously excited about the demo?"

"Yes, but she was always excited about her work, certainly whenever I'd spoken to her about it. That didn't make her any less professional, though."

"Do you know what she'd been doing in Sydney?"

"No."

"Do you think you could find out? Maybe talk to anyone she might have interacted with there?"

Alan nodded, probably pleased at the prospect of having something to do. "Sure." He gestured towards the door. "Shall I...?"

"No, hang on a second. There are still some things I want to run past you." I considered for a moment. "This demo. Would you personally have been able to sign Scott's paycheck, here and now, if things had panned out?"

"Theoretically, yes. Although, depending upon the price tag, I may have had to tap sources further up the line. Assuming I felt it was worth it."

"And…what's your gut feeling? Do you think that whatever-it-was would have been worth extra payment if Scott had asked for it?"

Alan grimaced and spread his hands wide. "I mean, she'd told us absolutely nothing about the specific nature of the project."

"But you must have had an existing interest in her work to be allocating funding. So, educated guess?"

Alan shrugged. "She'd always delivered in the past."

I didn't quite roll my eyes. Getting information out of Alan was beginning to feel like trying to extract a tooth using my fingers: slow and painful. "Right. So she'd done work for you before."

Samedi grinned. "Oh, indeed, Sah! Yes, indeed!"

I gave Alan a look. "So what was her focus of research?"

Alan shuffled slightly, saying nothing.

"Oh, for fuck's sake! I know you don't want anyone knowing too much about this shit, but just give me the basics," I snapped. "Areas of expertise, general applications, that sort of thing. It's almost certainly important, and—" I pulled out my phone and glanced at the screen, "—we only have about four hours and counting…"

Alan sighed. "Okay, well, most of her work was in defence metallurgical research and design. Producing materials used in fast construction of military instalments. Support structures for bridges, oilfield equipment, deep sea projects, that sort of thing."

"Actual weapons, though?"

Alan shook his head emphatically. "No. These materials don't lend themselves to that."

"Okay. So, again, why is there a tank full of ballistics gel on the bench over there?"

"I honestly don't know. But she was a chemist in charge of her own private company, and certainly undertook research unrelated to the military, so maybe she was using it for a completely different project. Maybe ballistics gel has other applications than just firearms testing. I don't know."

"Okay, fair enough." I glanced hopefully at the cat.

"No idea," the cat admitted.

I glanced around the room again, and a thought occurred. "Alan, how many personnel were with you for this pitch?"

"Five. Not including myself. Why?"

"So, six military personnel, plus Scott, plus—"

I looked over at the champagne tray. Seven glasses. Hubby hadn't been invited. Which could simply mean that Scott had intended this strictly as a work thing. Or...

"Okay," I said. "Colonel, if you could start making some calls about Scott's Sydney trip, that'd be great."

"On it," said Alan. "What are you going to do?"

"I think I'll have a chat with Mister Scott," I said.

"Prendergast."

"I'm sorry?"

Scott's husband tilted his head back, so that even from his seated position he could look down his nose at me. "My *wife's* surname was Scott. *Mine* is Prendergast."

Was. This guy had already relegated his wife to the past. A small yellow video-game star spun cheerily above Prendergast's shoulder in stark contrast to his own cold demeanour. He was balding, with what hair remained clearly and rather inexpertly dyed brown; oversized fashion spectacles, expression like he'd just sucked a lemon, full suit and tie. It all combined to make him look like an insufferable twat. I did my best to remember that *twat* didn't necessarily mean *guilty*.

"My apologies, no offence intended," I assured him. "And I'm genuinely sorry to burden you at what's obviously a very difficult time, but I do need to ask you—"

"As I've explained to every other cretin today," Prendergast snapped, "I won't be discussing anything with anyone except for my lawyer."

I caught the eye of the military guard standing beside Prendergast's chair. Her expression was professionally neutral, although the bluebird on her shoulder was giving me a distinct *If you don't punch him, I will* look.

"Right. Well. That's a shame," I said, "because—as I believe has been explained to you already—for the moment the only lawyer you have a right to is the lawyer assigned to you by Colonel Cook. A right that you've waived, I note. So, given that you are literally the only current suspect in your wife's murder, you may actually find that answering my questions is very much in your interests."

"Assuming that you *didn't* kill your wife, that is," the cat added.

A tiny smile touched the edge of Prendergast's sneer. The effect was highly unpleasant. "I'm not saying anything. And when you are finally compelled to release me due to lack of evidence, I will sue you for everything you own. My lawyer will tear each and every one of you to shreds."

I caught the bluebird's expression again. *We could make it look like an accident…*

"Excuse me a moment." I glanced at the cat. "Quick chat in private?" I asked, before realising the suggestion was redundant, as the animal would automatically and perpetually trail me wherever I went. I mentally cursed myself for making the slip in front of the oh-so-superior Prendergast; I still hadn't gotten a handle on including the cat in my investigation. We retreated sufficiently far away for Prendergast to be unable to overhear us. Which was a fair distance, as it happened.

They'd confined Prendergast to his own study, situated in the residential part of the house, and it was frankly huge: all dark wood and opulent leather, lush carpeting and armchairs, and bookshelves crammed with hardbacked volumes, many of which looked extremely old and valuable. A number of ornately framed paintings hung on the walls, and the heavy desk in the corner looked like it was probably a genuine antique. Victorian, maybe? A massive, well-lit aquarium, filled with a dizzying assortment of tropical fish, illuminated the far end of the room.

"Clearly guilty," the cat opined.

"Probably. But super confident that we can't pin anything on him."

"Well, hopefully he's wrong. It'd be nice to wipe that sneer off his face."

"Agreed." I leaned closer to the cat. "Look, um…I feel like I'm maybe getting a handle on…you."

"Oh, yes?"

"Yeah. It kinda seems like you notice all the same stuff that I would, only it takes slightly longer for those details to filter through to my conscious mind and percolate into something useful, whereas you process it all straight away."

"*Slightly* longer?"

"Don't be a dick. I'm complimenting you here."

The cat licked a paw daintily. "Okay."

"Is that a 'yes'?"

The cat shrugged.

"Well, what I'm wondering is, seeing as how Prendergast's refusing to spill, how much information do you think *you* could get out of him if *I* did all the talking?"

"Reading his body language, you mean? Facial tics, breathing, that sort of thing?" The cat peered past me to regard Prendergast. "I can give it a go. Keep in mind, though, anything I can tell you would legally be considered conjecture, not proof."

"Oh, I know, but if we can at least get a handle on the 'why,' then maybe we can get to the 'how' more quickly."

The cat shrugged again. "Sure, I'll give it a go."

"Just let me do the talking, okay?"

"You're the boss."

Prendergast deigned not to acknowledge us as we approached him again. "Sooooo, Mister Prendergast. How did you and your wife get along?" No answer. "What was the fight about? Can you tell me that?" I gave the cat a sidelong glance. "Financial issues? Maybe you felt she was spending too much time working?" No response. "Or maybe something more trivial. Someone left the cap off the toothpaste? Jealousy over one of you having a better aquarium display than the other?"

"Was she about to divorce you?" the cat interjected.

Even I saw Prendergast stiffen at that. I nodded, and unthinkingly beckoned the cat to follow me back into the corner of the room. "What happened to me doing the talking?"

"Sorry," the cat said. "It just seemed like an obvious question. You saw his reaction, though?"

"Oh, yes indeedy. Did you glean anything else from him?"

The cat scratched thoughtfully behind its ear. "Well, his breathing increased slightly when you asked about money. That's why I jumped in to ask about divorce."

"Okay. Makes sense he'd be worried about money if they're getting divorced. I wonder if she has a pre-nup? He certainly has more expensive tastes than I'd assume an academic's salary would support, although I could be wrong. Anything else?"

"Well, that crack you made about aquarium fish? I got a pretty strong reaction to that one as well."

"A worried reaction? Or something else?"

"Worried."

"Huh. Any ideas about that?"

The cat shook its head. "None whatsoever. Maybe we should pop back to Scott's workshop?"

"What, and check out her aquarium?"

The cat shrugged again.

Back in Scott's laboratory, with Delgado still working behind us (and John Lennon assisting by pointing out the spots she'd apparently failed to swab sufficiently), the cat and I peered through the front of the aquarium, which contained around a dozen pretty little blue-and-red fish, some aquatic plants, a jumble of small, rust-coloured rocks, and an ornament shaped like a sunken galleon sitting on the white gravel at the bottom, along with an aquarium heater stuck to the back wall of the tank. Nothing that struck me as significant. I glanced at the shelf above the tank. As I'd assumed, there was no indication of any music-sharing accounts on the stereo display, just the collection of CDs racked beside it. Mostly 80s and 90s Oz Rock, I noted: Baby Animals, Midnight Oil, The Living End, and so on. Music that a woman on her late forties might have listened to as a child, and possibly the actual albums she'd bought back then, judging from the worn state of the jewel cases. The digital picture frame beside the CDs was cycling through a number of photographs of presumed family and friends, as well as a few showing a younger Karen Scott—standing on a beach, drinking at a party, posing in front of a small home aquarium—and a far more recent pic of her posing next to the aquarium the cat and I now stood before.

"Check the stand?" the cat suggested.

I nodded, fishing a pair of latex gloves from the pocket of my coat. Pulling them on, I squatted down and opened the twin doors at the front of the stand. Inside was a small assembly of what I assumed was fairly basic aquarium equipment, as far as my limited knowledge of such things went. There was a softly-humming motor for the filtration system, a small open-top container that looked like it was being used as a bin, a small hand-held net, a container of fish food, and a small plastic box containing vials of aquarium chemicals.

"What's in the bin?" the cat asked.

I pulled the bin towards us. Inside were a few algae-encrusted cotton pads, of the sort used to remove makeup, and a clear, mid-sized plastic bag with a hole torn in one side, the top knotted with a rubber band. The sort of thing you'd bring aquarium fish home in.

"Bag's wet," the cat noted.

I peered at the brightly-coloured fish in the aquarium. "So something's been introduced to this tank within the last day or so. And since Scott only just returned from interstate, Prendergast must have done it." I glanced up at the digital frame. "Hey. These fish are different from the ones in the most recent picture," I noted, as the photograph in question briefly appeared again.

"Yeah, I noticed that too."

"Huh. Maybe I'm catching up with you."

The cat shrugged.

I stood and waited until the photograph of Scott in front of the aquarium reappeared, then paused the display cycle. "Yeah. Looks like ordinary goldfish in the photo. So, what are these?" I indicated the current residents of the tank.

"No idea. Might not even be relevant."

I pulled my phone out of my pocket. "Maybe it's relevant to the argument between Scott and Prendergast." I started Googling. "I think they might be neon tetras," I said eventually.

"Okay. So?" the cat asked.

"I'm not sure," I said slowly, "but..." I turned back towards Delgado, who had moved on to swabbing the sinks on the work bench. "Hey, Delgado? Did anybody search the aquarium?"

She shook her head. "No. We figured that if a weapon had been stashed there it'd be easily visible, and there's clearly nothing weapon-y in there."

"What if it'd been shoved under the gravel at the bottom?"

"The husband's hands and arms were dry, according to Colonel Cook." Delgado shrugged. "So..."

"Okay. Thanks." I stared through the front of the aquarium again. Dead end.

"Maybe...what if Scott was working on some sort of stealth tech?" the cat suggested. "Bends light, or something, so it's invisible to the naked eye?"

"Something that could be sitting right in front of us," I finished, nodding. "Yeah. But that line of investigation could be endless, and yield nothing. Although I guess a quick look at the specifics of her past work might at least give us a clue..." I Googled Scott's name. Found some articles. Started browsing. "Yeah, just like Alan said. She was researching new materials for use in construction. Bridge supports...oilfield equipment...deep sea projects..." I trailed off, frowning as I read further.

"What?" the cat asked eventually.

"Look." I showed the cat the article on my phoner screen. "There." I pointed. "The stuff about chemical reactions."

"Okay." The cat leaned in to peruse the indicated text. "So..." It read silently for a moment. "Hang on. Wait..."

We looked at one another. Then we both stared into the aquarium again.

And then, for both of us, it finally clicked.

"Oh, SHIT!" we yelled simultaneously.

"Delgado!" I called out, hurriedly bending to retrieve the net from the stand. "Do you have something I can use to dry off evidence??"

"Sure," Delgado said, as she and Lennon hurried over. "But what—?"

I turned to her, desperately shaking water from the rusty pebble-like objects I'd scooped up in the net. "Here! I need these fully dried out, right now!"

"Dried?"

"Bone dry! I dunno, put them under heat lamps, or something! If we can't get these dry, we're fucked!"

Suitably agitated by my demeanour, Delgado snatched the net from me and dashed away.

I turned back to the cat, trying to calm myself. "Okay. Okay."

"Are we absolutely sure about this?" the cat asked.

"Yep. I mean, maybe. I mean, I don't know," I gabbled. "But we couldn't afford to muck about. Now we just need to check all of the rubbish bins in this house, and the outside bins too, then Google the difference between keeping goldfish and tetras. And then we see what Alan has to tell us about Scott's interstate trip…"

"So?" I asked.

Alan glanced at the crusty collection of physical evidence I'd taken from the aquarium, now spread out across a sheet of plastic underneath a hastily-rigged heat lamp, looking more like a scattering of oxidised sandstone pebbles than shale. Slight wisps of steam still curled up from a couple of the larger pieces. The bin and chemical kit from the aquarium stand sat alongside "What the hell is all this?" He looked over at Delgado and Lennon.

"Evidence?" Lennon ventured.

"Which we'll get to in a moment," I said. "What did you find out about Scott's trip?"

"Um… Okay, well, she was up in Sydney for eight days. It's where she grew up. Spent much of her trip catching up with friends. Lunches, bars, a couple of nights out on the town. That sort of thing."

"Did you talk to any of those friends? How did they say she seemed?"

Alan shrugged. "They were all obviously shocked by the news of her murder, so it was hard to coax much cohesive information from any of them, but it seems like she was a rather different person outside of her working environment. You tend to think people will be more businesslike at work and emotional in their personal life, but Scott was apparently the opposite, always excited about work in general but more cool and calm during her downtime. Her friends describe her as being laid-back, even when partying, but not in a demonstrative or excitable way."

"Did she happen to consult a lawyer about divorcing Prendergast?" the cat asked.

"How—?"

"Did she?" I pressed.

"Well, yes. Couple of meetings. Flew back here with papers ready to serve to Prendergast."

"Why would she fly to Sydney to file for divorce?"

"Well, the lawyer just happened to be one of the longtime friends she'd gone up to socialise with, so I guess it was partly a matter of convenience."

"Hm. Did Scott experience any delays coming back from Sydney?"

Alan actually looked impressed. "She only got back this morning, after her scheduled flight last night got cancelled due to crappy Melbourne weather. I suppose that's why she was still rushing around to set up the demo when my team arrived today."

"Right. Right." I exchanged a glance with the cat. "Right."

"What—?" Alan began, but the cat shooshed him.

"Give him a moment. He's percolating."

"He's what now?"

"Percolating," Samedi echoed. "Like a fine coffee, Boss. All the elements coming together."

"Okay, then." Alan gave me a hard stare, which I ignored.

I steepled my fingers in front of my face, thinking, pacing slowly back and forth. Thinking some more. "Okay." I said eventually, rubbing my hands together. "I think I've cracked it."

The cat coughed politely.

I gave the cat a look, then nodded slowly. "Yeah. Okay, *We* cracked it. Together. But it's a pretty long explanation, and not completely linear, so stay with me on this, okay? And no interruptions, because it's all still percolating."

Alan and Samedi both pulled identical expressions of impatience.

"Okay," I said again. "So, first clue was the fish in the aquarium. We figure Scott asked Prendergast to look after her goldfish while she was away. Feed them, etcetera. But while Prendergast shared her interest in fish, he didn't really give a crap about following her instructions. The marriage was already pretty rocky by this point, for various reasons that actually aren't relevant. Most of it boils down to slow estrangement from one another due to increasingly different values and goals, although Prendergast doesn't seem to have suspected that Scott was preparing to divorce him. So anyway, he neglected the fish, and they died."

"Which a quick search of the outside bin confirmed," the cat added. "It was pretty rank. But helpful for us that he didn't simply flush them away."

"We found a torn plastic bag under the aquarium," I continued, pointing to the bin on the bench, "and realised that Prendergast had replaced all the fish within just the last couple of days."

"Except that he chose the wrong fish," the cat said.

"See, all the personal stuff Scott kept in here was for nostalgic reasons. The music she loved as a kid, photographs, even the goldfish, because she'd also kept them as a child. But Prendergast isn't nostalgic like that. He just wants the best of everything. Trophies. So when he replaced the goldfish, he replaced them with what he considered to be *better* fish. Neon tetras. More sparkly and exotic-looking. Not from his own aquarium, of course. Those are *his*. He went out and bought new ones, along with an aquarium heater, which you don't need for plain old goldfish."

Alan nodded. "And that's what the argument was about?"

I held up a finger. "Yes, but not for the reasons you think. It wasn't the goldfish *per se* she was angry about. But we'll come back to that."

The cat stretched. "See, from what you've said, Scott was very calm when dealing with personal issues. It was work matters that made her emotional. Ergo, Scott's anger in this case was work-related."

"Okay," Alan said, looking nonplussed.

"So," the cat continued, "stick a pin in that for the moment, and let's consider the demo Scott was planning for you. The ballistic gel block over there indicates the demo definitely involved a weapon, despite your assertion that her field of expertise had no applications in actual weaponry. And it seemed fair to assume the demo weapon was the same one used to kill Scott. A weapon that then apparently vanished into thin air."

"So, I started Googling Scott's previous work," I said, "hoping to get some hints about what sort of weapon she might have been developing." I gave Alan a stern look. "Why didn't you mention her specific area of expertise was in dissolvable metals?"

Alan gave me a blank look. "Well, because…I mean, it didn't seem relevant."

"Why not?"

Alan shrugged. "What? You're suggesting that Scott made some sort of firearm out of dissolvable metal, and Prendergast killed her with it, then disposed of it in the aquarium?"

"That doesn't seem obvious to you?"

"Well, no. As I've explained, the materials Scott produced were used to create support structures for military developments."

"Sure," I interrupted, "but more specifically she created materials used to build *short-term* support structures. So a deep-sea base, for example, could be built in record time using Scott's metal to support concrete or other materials that were still curing or settling, after which those supports would dissolve away, leaving behind a fully functional and accessible structure, yes?"

Alan was looking increasingly frustrated. Even Samedi was starting to give me the evil eye. "Yes, okay, but we're talking about really thick metal, dense metal. It takes *weeks* for supports like that to dissolve in water, if not months. In fact, you need a heavy nitric acid solution to dissolve even a small piece of this metal more quickly, and even then it can take anything from several hours to a full day."

The cat blinked. "I'm impressed you know that much about the process."

"I do actually look into these things before throwing money at them, you know."

"Okay," I pressed, "but what if you used 3D printing or some such to produce really thin pieces of dissolvable metal?"

"I can see where you are taking this, Sah," Samedi intoned, "but any 3D-printed weapon strong enough to survive being fired would require a solution *faaaaar* more acidic than aquarium water in which to dissolve."

"Unless that weapon was intended as a single-use firearm," the cat said, nodding towards the corroded debris spread across the bench.

"*That* is what's left of Scott's weapon. It's obviously in pretty poor condition, but a forensic team can probably confirm it, thanks to our quick action in hauling it out of the tank. And Delgado's speed in setting up the heat lamps."

Alan pressed his fingers to his temples, as though warding off a headache. "But…how did it deteriorate so fast?"

"Okay," I said. "So, if the cat and I are right—"

"Hurrah! I got credited!" the cat purred.

"—and I'm pretty damn certain we are," I continued, "Scott hit upon the idea of a single-use, water-soluble firearm, something that could be used for, say, assassinations, and then disposed of quickly. So she created a metal alloy that was sufficiently strong to hold together during the firing process while also being thin enough to retain the ability to dissolve, probably by adding something like titanium to the 3D printing process. Again, forensics can confirm that. She also licked the issue of the metal taking ages to dissolve by developing a mix that could dissolve within minutes rather than hours, and I'll come back to that in a moment," I added, as Alan opened his mouth to interject.

"So," the cat said, picking up where I'd left off, "Scott organises the demo. And with the promise of a massive payout looming, she decides that this is the perfect time to organise her divorce. She flies out to Sydney, parties a bit, organises the papers, then heads back to town, arrives late due to the flight cancellation, and because she's scrabbling to get the demo ready she only notices at the last moment that one major element of the demo has been utterly screwed up."

"The fish," I added. "Or rather, the aquarium. And yes, we'll get to that in a moment."

"You keep saying that," Alan snapped. "Is there any danger of getting to the point of all this?"

I held up my hands. "I warned you this was going to be a long and winding road. But it's important for you to have the complete picture so you can communicate our findings to the judge."

Alan glanced at his watch. "Talk faster."

"Okay," I said. "So Scott confronts Prendergast about the issue, flies into a rage, and almost certainly loses her cool sufficiently to blurt out that she's kicking him to the kerb. Now, I imagine a man with expensive tastes like Prendergast would already have been in a pretty foul mood when he realised he was going to be missing out on a glass of finest bubbly." I nodded towards the tray on the bench. "There are only enough glasses for Scott and your team, so it's obvious he was the one person in the house being excluded. It may not have been a deliberate snub, but it doesn't really matter. He would have been angry about it, and when Scott revealed that he was about to be cut off from the comfortable lifestyle to which he'd become accustomed, which I'm sure had been funded by Scott as the primary breadwinner—let alone from the impending fortune from Scott's military contract—he flew into an absolute rage."

"He's an absolute foaming shitgibbon, is what we're saying," the cat interjected helpfully.

Alan and I both nodded agreement.

"Anyway," I pressed, "Prendergast snatches the prototype off the bench here, shoots Scott in the head, then dashes over to the aquarium and drops the gun in."

"So he understood the properties of the weapon," Alan stated.

"Some," the cat agreed. "Enough to know the weapon was supposed to dissolve in water. Assuming he wasn't already privy to the basic details of his wife's work, Scott may have clued him in during the argument when she tried to explain why she was so angry, which was because she'd been going to dissolve the gun in the aquarium as part of the demo, and Prendergast had gone and fucked it all up."

"He probably thought she was just being precious about the fish," I concluded, "and shot her before she could explain in more detail, which is why he was so confident that the gun would dissolve too quickly for us to ever find." I gave Alan a look. "Which leaves us with two final questions. Firstly, why did Prendergast's replacement of the goldfish lead to a work-related argument with Scott, and secondly, what happened to the bullet that killed Scott?"

Alan sighed. "Go on, then. You're obviously dying to impress me." He glanced at the cat. "Both of you."

The cat preened. "So, the issue with making these metals dissolve *fast* is the need for nitric acid. Fortunately, if you can't immerse it in acid, you can pump an acid gel through the microstructures of the metal." The cat winked at Alan. "Google is our friend."

"Problem is," I continued, "an assassin looking to dispose of a murder weapon isn't likely to have access to nitric acid. So Scott developed a metal that could dissolve rapidly in *any* liquid, so long as the pH—that is, the acidity—was within a certain narrow range, the end result being an alloy that dissolved super quickly—like, in minutes—in…wait for it…"

"Drumroll please!" the cat purred.

"…regular old drinking water! Which most of us have access to, and—fun fact—generally has a pH of seven."

Alan raised his eyebrows. "That's brilliant if true. You could dispose of a weapon like that in a sink, or a toilet." He frowned again. "But the water in the aquarium took hours to reduce the weapon to *that* state." He indicated the remains on the bench. "So why did Prendergast dispose of it there instead of chucking it into one of these sinks, which are closer to where he shot Scott?" He indicated a nearby sink on the workbench.

"Good question," I said. "For starters, if you'd busted in here and seen the tap running, that would have alerted your attention to the sink before the weapon could dissolve. But I don't think Prendergast actually considered that. As a result of whatever Scott told him during the argument, I think Prendergast already had in his head that the aquarium was going to be used in the demo to show your team how easily the weapon could be disposed of. Of course, we also know that he didn't have sufficient info to realise that it wouldn't work—but I'll come back to that. So, in that moment of panic after he killed Scott, he automatically ran to the aquarium and dropped the gun in behind the ornaments and plants, where ideally it would have gone unnoticed while it dissolved completely within minutes. Which is exactly the demo Scott had planned for your team."

"So why didn't anyone on my team see it when we started searching the room?" Alan demanded.

"*Because* the outer surface of the gun would have discoloured almost immediately, and by the time your guys started actually sweeping the room for the weapon—which I'm guessing would have been at least a few minutes after the murder, given the time you would have taken to secure Prendergast, check Scott to see if she was alive, and then call it all in—there would already have been sufficient corrosion on the surface of the weapon to make it look…" I shrugged, "…not like a weapon anymore. By that time it probably already just looked like what me and the cat thought it was. A decorative rock."

"So why hadn't it completely dissolved by the time you identified it?"

"Cat?" I prompted.

The cat nodded. "Going back to the issue of the fish, different species require water with different pH. Goldfish, for example, love a pH of around seven. The same as—"

"Drinking water," finished Alan, a spark of understanding in his eyes. "Holy crap!"

"Exactly! But when Prendergast replaced the goldfish with neon tetras, which he knew preferred a pH of around five-point-five, he added an alkaline solution to the water," the cat nodded towards the box of aquarium chemicals sitting on the bench, "not realising it was going to ruin Scott's demo. But Scott realised it as soon as she noticed the goldfish had gone, which wasn't until a few minutes before the demo was scheduled. She flies into a rage, tells Prendergast he's out on his ear, and gets shot for it."

Alan and Samedi both nodded wonderingly. "Wow. That's…wow," Alan said. "Holy crap. So the water was still acidic enough for the metal to dissolve…just not sufficiently to make it happen *fast*."

"Luckily for us."

"But what about the bullet, my friend?" Samedi urged. "The human head is not filled with drinking water, after all!"

"No," the cat said. "But would you like to guess what the pH of human blood is?"

"Unbelievable," Alan murmured, then he frowned again. "But Prendergast must have known we had the rights to Scott's work, and that we'd find all the relevant information about the gun when we looked at her notes, which would have proved what he did with the murder weapon."

"Circumstantial," the cat said. "By the time you twigged, the gun would be long gone, and any residue found in the tank could have been explained away as having come from past experiments by Scott. And as for you taking ownership of Scott's work after her death, I'm assuming your contract would instruct payment for that work to go to her family instead, and—"

"And Scott was still married to Prendergast, despite having drawn up the divorce papers," Alan finished, shaking his head. "And if she'd had a chance to divorce him, I'm assuming whatever pre-nup they had in place wouldn't have provided anywhere near as big a payday as our contract would." A tinge of anger crossed his face. "So, wait, was this a crime of passion, or did he actually take a moment to consider his options, even if it was on the fly? Can they get him on premeditation?" Alan noted my expression of surprise at his anger. "She always seemed like a nice lady," he explained curtly.

I shrugged. "Maybe. That'll be up to the courts to decide. But I doubt he'll be making any money from this either way. Maybe the military payout will go to more distant family."

Alan exhaled noisily. "Yeah. Okay. Well, I think we have more than enough to take to the judge to get Prendergast charged, and to secure our jurisdiction of the crime scene and Scott's work." He glanced at his watch. "I'd better run, though. Delgado? Can you bag everything up, please?"

"Can do."

"Want us to come with?" I asked.

Alan paused, considering. "Not just yet, no. I mean, we'll get around to all the paperwork you'll need to sign off on. And I'll action the commission fee as soon as I get back to the office, with full payment once the judge rules the case closed, yeah?"

I nodded. The commission fee alone would keep me in comfort for an exceptionally long time. "Cool."

"Besides, Sah," Samedi added, "the Boss will be talking 'shop' with the judge, to hasten access to Scott's work. Sensitive information being discussed, yes?" He winked.

I nodded. "Palms to be greased."

Alan gave Samedi a stern look. Samedi laughed. "Just so, my friend. Just so."

Alan extended his hand. "Thanks, Jim."

We shook. "You're welcome," I said, and meant it.

I leaned back against the bench with a sigh as Alan and Samedi left.

"You look happy," the cat observed.

"Yeah," I admitted. "It felt good. Not just having a case after so long, but dealing with a case that actually presented a real challenge."

"Massive paycheck doesn't hurt, either."

"It does not," I agreed.

We ruminated in silence for a moment.

"So, listen," I began.

"Mm?"

"Just…thanks for everything. Y'know? I mean, frankly, I still suspect you're a projection of my subconscious. But even if that's true, even if I really am basically just talking to myself, so to speak, then it doesn't make much sense to be…y'know…"

"Treating me like utter shit?"

I winced. "Yeah. That. So, y'know. Sorry."

"Apology accepted," the cat said. "Only…"

"What?"

"Well, what if I am, in fact, a magical, immaterial, talking cat?"

I shrugged. "Well, either way, you were really helpful today. It would have taken me more time than we'd been given to put all the pieces together, and maybe not even then. We might not even have found the remaining gun fragments in time if you hadn't helped to lead me down the trail that led us there. So, thanks."

"My pleasure." The cat stretched luxuriously. "Soooo…in lieu of payment for my services, how about giving me a name?"

I blinked. "Um. Yeah. Sure. Any preferences?"

"I quite like…Coco."

"Cool. Coco it is, then."

The cat—*Coco*, I corrected myself—nodded. "Yay. It has a nice ring to it, don't you think?"

"Coco the Cat. Yeah, I guess."

"No. Well, yes, that too. But I meant 'Coco and Carpenter'."

"Whut?"

"You know, on the door of our office."

I gave Coco a look. "Let's not get ahead of ourselves. A name is the best you get out of me for the moment."

Coco shrugged. "Fair. How about 'Carpenter and Cat'?"

I sighed. "That'll do, cat. That'll do."

Ten Tales of Astounding Science Fiction

1

"Does my bum look big in this?"

He glanced at her. "Well, yes. But I *like* women with big bums."

"Great!" she beamed. "In that case, I'm ready to go…"

2

As always, every available bank teller was on duty, so Steve found himself at the head of the queue in no time.

3

"I'm so sorry to be running late," the bus driver apologised as Gwen got on. "The traffic's always awful at this time of the morning. But that's no excuse, really—we should be planning the timetable better to work around the predictable delays, shouldn't we?"

Gwen waved off the apology as a number of young men rose to offer their seats. "Please don't feel bad. Honestly, it seems silly to get upset over such a small thing. I mean, it was only ten minutes…"

4

After slipping on a tricky patch of pavement near his home, Tom immediately sent off an extremely constructive email to his local council, alerting them to the problem and suggesting some practical solutions. Within twenty-four hours he received a phone call from the council, thanking him sincerely for his input, and informing him that several of his ideas were already being put into practice…

5

True to his word, the plumber arrived at exactly 10.30 a.m.

6

"Definitely the alternator," the mechanic said. "Luckily I've got a spare one out the back. Glad to find a use for it. Call it…twenty bucks for labour and I'll throw in the part for nothing, seeing as it was just sitting around gathering dust. If you've got time to wait, the entire job shouldn't take more than half-an-hour..."

7

"So," he said hesitantly. "Do you, er, want to cuddle? Talk a little? You don't have to go right away, do you?"

"Sorry," she said, throwing back the sheets. "You know how it is. Anyway, I was really just after a good, hard—"

8

The nineteen-year-old sales assistant immediately stopped conversing with her coworker as Jenny entered the boutique, and offered a genuine smile. "Hello there! What can I help you with today?"

9

"Well, I've got no bloody idea where we are," he said. "Hang on—I'll just pull over and look at the map."

10

"The machine *worked*, Susan! I made the jump—*right into an alternate version of our world!*" Dean gazed up painfully from his hospital bed. "And…it was *awful!* A *twisted* version! People in power imposing wars and sanctions upon those least able to defend themselves! Whole nations starving while others produce more food than they can possibly consume! Children being sexually abused, or sold like appliances! The have-nots being forced further into debt and despair by the haves! White-collar criminals receiving harsher punishments than rapists and murderers! Sexism! Racism! Overpopulation! Animal cruelty! Environmental vandalism!" His voice rose to a shout as he struggled to sit up. "And everyone is *so mean!*"

"Shh!" She pressed a hand against his sweating brow, and he fell back against the sheets, panting. "Dean, the technicians examined the remains of the machine very carefully. There's absolutely no evidence that it ever worked. You must have had some sort of…mental break. Or bumped your head. Or…" she shrugged apologetically, "maybe you just imagined it all."

"*No!*" He shook his head weakly. "It was *real!* A nightmare world!"

"Yes," she said quietly. "Only a nightmare…"

Incident at Five Mile Creek

1880, Bushland South-West of Glenrowan…

"Dammit, I said no!" Ned shouted, slamming a fist against the doorframe. "Are you out of your bloody *mind?*"

Dan cringed, half-expecting the decrepit bushman's hut to come crashing down under the force of his brother's anger. "Come on, Ned," he protested. "This is Kelly Country! They're givin' away your photograph with every daily paper! Most of the gold-diggers hereabouts would probably give their eye teeth just to ride with you!"

Steve nodded his agreement. "That's right, Ned. So why don't we ride into Oxley and see if we can't add a few dozen bodies to the gang?"

Ned swung around, his face glowing red through thick, black whiskers. "*Because*, you bloody fools, for every hundred who'd ride with us there's as many who'd see us all hang! Tell 'em, Joe!"

Joe regarded Ned thoughtfully. "An eight-thousand pound reward's a powerful incentive to turn us all in. Can't argue with that. Although if we did do some recruiting—and Dan's right about that, Ned, we do need more members—I reckon we're all smart enough to spot a nark." He paused. "But even if there are folks out there who'd shop us just for the thrill of it, you've never worried about what people like that think, Ned. So what's *really* got you so worked up?"

The others held their breath. Ned's respect for Joe—for his education, friendship, and loyalty—generally knew no bounds. But they'd never before seen Ned in such a foul mood, and wondered if perhaps Joe hadn't overstepped the mark.

For a moment Ned looked ready to explode. Then the anger seemed to drain from him, and he leaned heavily against the doorframe. "It's no good, Joe," he muttered. "They've set the trackers on us now. A white man stands no chance against those black buggers—they can track you over bare stone!"

Joe nodded. The native trackers had been trailing the gang relentlessly across the state for the past month, and Ned had developed an almost superstitious fear of them. The bushman's hut offered a few nights' shelter at best, then they would have to move on. But the net was beginning to tighten, and they could all feel it. They couldn't outrun the troopers forever, and it was only a matter of time before they would have to make a stand.

"Nah," Dan blustered, without much conviction, "blackfellas are just men. No magic—no guns, even. If they do track us down it'll be up to the pigs to take us on, and we can lick 'em easy!"

In spite of himself, Ned smiled. "Yeah, well... Maybe we should start trackin' the trackers, eh? If we could pick 'em off, that'd leave the troopers at a loose end."

Dan smirked. "They're already at a loose end, I reckon." This drew a round of appreciative laughter from the others. "I mean, look at 'em! They're gettin' really desperate now, firin' off cannons at night on the off chance they'll hit us."

Ned's grin vanished. "What? What are you talkin' about?"

"Didn't you hear 'em? Last night?"

"Wouldn't ask if I had, would I?"

Dan glanced around at the others, seeking support.

Steve shrugged. "I mean...I heard *something*. Thought it was thunder at first, a big rolling sound overhead, and then a sort of whooshing like heavy rain, only there weren't any rain. But then there was another big bang, like an explosion, much closer. Thought it might be someone mining, but it was too clear. Like, not muffled by being underground, y'know?" He shot Dan a dubious look. "Dunno about a cannon though. I mean, how would anyone get a cannon all the way out into the bushland here? Even the horses had trouble getting' through the scrub, so…"

Ned glanced at Joe, eyebrows raised.

Joe nodded reluctantly. "Yeah. I heard it. Figured it was someone doing some blasting, but I suppose it could have been a cannon. Came from a way off—somewhere further up Five Mile Creek, I reckon. Maybe a few miles."

Ned glared at each of his companions in turn. "And it never occurred to any of you bloody idiots to mention this to *me*? What if they've been getting' closer all this time?" He grabbed his revolvers from the table, checked that they were loaded, then thrust them into his belt. "I'm gunna ride up along the creek bed and take a look."

Dan leapt to his feet. "Wait, Ned—we'll come with you!"

"No! If it *is* the law, they'll prob'ly be watchin' the area to see if they've stirred us up."

"Well, if that's so, you'll need our help!"

Ned grinned savagely. "They'll be expectin' four of us—not a single rider. If I spot 'em, I can be away before they spot me. And even if they do spot me, one of us can bolt through the scrub easier than a bunch of us." He stepped forward and clapped Dan on the shoulder. "Stay alert, and get the horses loaded. You need to be ready to run, just in case." Dan nodded reluctantly. Ned gave his brother's shoulder a final squeeze, then headed toward the door. "If I'm not back by nightfall, go to Mother's. She'll know what to do."

That summer had been a hot one, but the dependable flow of Five Mile Creek had kept the vegetation on the banks well-watered. Here and there, sinkholes had been gouged out of the lower banks by the constant motion of the water, filled with viscous, ochre mud dredged up from the creek bed. Ned kept a wary eye on these as his horse trotted along the bank; a big sinkhole could be worse than quicksand, capable of dragging man or beast down into the ooze. With the other eye, Ned scanned the trees fringing the creek. The well-spaced, straggly ghost gums offered little in the way of cover for an ambush but, in lieu of anything better, that was where the troopers would be hiding. If they were there at all, of course.

It was not knowing for sure that really got to Ned. As if he didn't have enough to worry about already; running from the trackers, taking responsibility for the safety of his brother and the others. And now the pressures of leadership had him jumping at noises in the night. If it did turn out to be troopers—well, fine. He would deal with it. But until he found out for sure, one way or the other, he'd be jumpy as all hell, and that could be dangerous in itself, distracting him from—

Abruptly, the horse gave a shrill cry and jerked to a halt, almost spilling Ned from the saddle. Ned swore, raising his hand to cuff the animal…then stopped abruptly.

What in blazes—?

They had reached an area perhaps two miles from the hut, where the thick bush along the bank Ned was traversing gave way to open farmland. And here, something strange had occurred. The vegetation was queerly blackened on both sides of the creek; not the crisp, charcoal black of a bushfire, more a thin coating of grey ash, as though a momentary wave of incredible heat had flared out from the creek bed. Acrid smoke still drifted from the burnt scrub, the horse continuing to complain as its eyes watered. An explosion? Cannon-fire? That didn't make sense. No cannon shot would create such weird burn-marks. And there would have been more percussive damage; trees shattered into matchsticks, clay banks opened up and drying in the sun. Instead, maybe fifty yards further up the creek, a single massive furrow emerged from the bushland to Ned's left, completely bisecting the creek bed— the banks on both sides torn open, with the trees and brush flanking the gaping wound uprooted and fallen, though no more damaged than that—then ploughing on into the neighbouring field for a distance of maybe two-hundred yards, stopping just short of a large graziers' water tower.

Ned eyed the scene suspiciously, his natural sense of caution warring with a burning curiousity. To venture out into the field meant leaving the cover of the trees and the bank. If there were troopers about he'd be spotted immediately, and would present an easy target besides. Then again, the field offered little in the way of cover for an ambush. And if that furrow *had* been caused by trooper activities, it would be to Ned's advantage to find out more about it.

Finally deciding in favour of curiousity, Ned urged his horse up the side of the bank and out into the field beyond, the animal stumbling nervously along the edge of the furrow until they reached a shallow crater at the end. And there they stopped, the horse whickering and pulling against its bit.

Ned understood exactly how the horse felt.

Lying in the crater was a huge, cigar-shaped object—perhaps the size of a locomotive engine—almost entirely coated with dried mud, except for a few spots where a weird, shining metal glittered between gaps in the filth.

Ned's horse pawed the ground, huffing restlessly. It was only then that Ned realised how quiet it was. The splash from a clump of soil that suddenly tumbled down the crater wall and landed in the pool of water in which the cylinder lay seemed as loud and sudden as gunfire, and Ned flinched before he could stop himself.

Get a grip, Ned!

He took a deep breath, staring in wonder at the thing in the crater. What on Earth *was* it? A weapon of some kind? *Impossible! You'd need a cannon the size of a town to fire such a projectile!* And yet, the furrow indicated that the thing must have flown through the air at high speed before hitting the ground. So, if not fired from a cannon, how had the cylinder become airborne? Ned frowned. There had to be some sort of logical explanation. After all, the damned thing couldn't have simply fallen out of the sky.

Ned nudged his horse into motion, circumnavigating the crater. As he approached the opposite side he saw that the nearer end of the cylinder, tilting at an upwards angle against the wall of the crater, was *open*—a dark aperture, gaping up at the sky. Moving closer, Ned cautiously peered into the interior of the cylinder. It was completely hollow, as far as he could see, although admittedly the sunlight only penetrated a little way inside. Beyond was only blackness. An explosive projectile would have been filled with powder, so the thing obviously couldn't be a weapon. Unless, of course, it had contained something *other* than explosives. Men, perhaps? Was this some sort of weird new transport, used for inserting troopers into difficult terrain?

Ned shook his head. *Fantasy*, he thought. *Get your head out of the clouds, Ned—you couldn't put a man in that! Why, the impact of landing'd flatten him in an instant!*

And yet…

Ned glanced over at the nearby water tower. It was one of the biggest he'd ever seen, maybe 160 feet tall, and Ned figured that if he climbed to the top he would have an excellent view of the surrounding countryside. If there were any troopers nearby, he'd be sure to spot them.

Ned spurred his horse forward, heading toward the water tower at a gallop.

And at that moment the water tower turned and *looked* at him.

For a moment, Ned didn't understand what he was seeing. He brought his horse to an abrupt stop, gaping as the water tower lifted one of its struts and took a single, enormous step forward. Panicked, the horse reared and tried to bolt. Swearing, Ned wrestled with the reins, holding the petrified beast steady as he regarded the monstrous *thing* moving toward him.

It was, Ned suddenly realised, some sort of astounding mechanism. A gleaming hood, apparently crafted from the same metal as the cylinder, mounted upon a great, mobile tripod like a gigantic billy stand. Long, articulated metal ropes hung down from underneath the hood, writhing fitfully like the tentacles of some deep-sea creature, and atop the hood two pitch-black circles of what appeared to be glass peered balefully at Ned like the eye-sockets of a human skull.

ALOOOOOOOOOOOOO!

Ned felt the hairs on the back of his neck stand on end. The sound, clearly emanating from the tripod, was cold and pitiless and unlike anything he had ever heard before; an unearthly baying that rolled across the field like thunder. The horse struggled frantically against Ned's grip on the reins. Frozen with fear, Ned was dimly aware of his bladder letting go, the spreading warmth in his crotch doing little to counteract the chill in his veins.

The tripod bellowed again. Its two back legs swung forward—the entire mechanism balancing precariously on a single support for a moment—then slammed to the ground fifty yards closer to where Ned sat atop his horse.

At that, Ned's paralysis broke. Holding the reins steady with one hand he scrabbled at his belt with the other, pulling forth one of his Colt pistols, which he levelled at one of the tripod's great black eyes before pulling the trigger. The report of the pistol was followed instantly by a loud metallic *ping!* Ned blinked. He'd hit the thing squarely with a shot that would have punched a hole right through corrugated iron, let alone glass—he *knew* he had!—and yet, he couldn't see even a scratch on the thing!

Unfortunately, lack of damage notwithstanding, the tripod clearly wasn't going to allow Ned's attack to remain unpunished. A single great tentacle swung up into the air, reaching out toward Ned with what the bushranger could only assume was murderous intent.

Thrusting the Colt back into his belt, Ned pulled hard on the reins, swinging his horse around and spurring it into a gallop back toward the creek. He heard a deep *THUD!* behind him as the tripod presumably took another step forwards, but he resisted the urge to look back. Then came another thud. And another. Only when his horse burst through the tree line and reached the relative cover of the creek bank did Ned feel sufficiently secure to glance over his shoulder. To his horror, the tripod was little more than fifty yards behind him, and still gaining as it took one mighty step after another, the three legs swinging back and forth in a disjointed yet oddly graceful motion. Kicking desperately, Ned urged his mount forward at breakneck speed along the bank, cutting perilously close to several large sinkholes as they went. Another deep thud came from behind, so close this time that Ned felt the impact through his horse. He risked another glance backwards, and yelled in desperation. The tripod had stepped through the tree line on to the bank, and was virtually on top of him, the two back feet raising themselves to take a stride that would surely crush both rider and mount into the mud.

Ned yanked the reins, steering his horse from the bank and back out through the trees. If he couldn't outrun the hellish thing, perhaps he could give it the run-around until it gave up and stopped pursuing him. Out of the corner of his eye, he could see the tripod towering above the treetops, flanking him as it strode along the bank. Unsettlingly, its hood was turned toward him, staring unblinkingly with those two great 'eyes,' despite Ned moving at right angles to its passage. A second later one of its tentacles lashed out, and a mighty ghost gum to Ned's right shattered into kindling. With no discernible break in its stride, the tripod stepped through the resulting gap in the tree line and back on to the bank beside its quarry. Ned jerked back on the reins, forcing his horse to a stumbling halt, and the tripod shot past with the speed of a locomotive. With a savage yell of triumph, Ned swung his horse off to the right, back out through the tree line, and took off again at top speed.

For a moment, the tripod seemed to have lost its prey. It took several more giant strides before grinding to a complete halt. The great hood slowly rotated right around—*like the head of gigantic owl*, Ned thought—clearly attempting to find Ned again, until it once again faced in the direction of the fleeing rider. But by now Ned had a strong lead; another few moments and he would reach the point where open pasture became heavy bushland again, from where he reckoned he could easily give this overgrown billycan the slip. The bush would give him some valuable cover, and—if he could get across to the other side of the creek—there were several nearby gullies that would further slow the tripod down, if not halt it altogether. And if *that* didn't work—well, Ned knew of a number of caves hereabouts, some previously used by the blackfellas, where a hunted man could hole up until the coast was clear.

With another mighty yell, Ned dug his heels hard into his horse's flank. The poor beast was foaming at the mouth, eyes bulging as its hooves thundered along the bank. But Ned had little time for sympathy—he could worry about the horse once he was safely back at the hut. Until then—

OOOOOOOLAAAAAAAAAAAAAAAAA!

The thing sounded angry. *Good!* Ned thought, glancing back. The tripod hadn't moved, but was still glaring balefully in his direction. Two of its tentacles had stretched up in front of the hood, assuming a posture like that of a man praying, and Ned caught a glimpse of some shiny object clasped between the tips. Perhaps the machine had found something else to amuse itself with—abandoned farm equipment, or some such. *And welcome to it*, Ned thought, turning his back upon the rapidly receding mechanism.

WHOOOSH!

A blast of immense heat swept over Ned, as though a nearby furnace door had been flung open. At the same instant, a tree barely ten yards ahead exploded into flames. Ned gasped in the suffocating heat. *God! What sort of sorcery—?*

Ned decided that he really didn't want to find out. He dug his heels in again, urging his panicked mount forward at top speed, past the incinerated tree. Up ahead he could see where a huge tree root had grown across the creek bed, a platform of mud and debris caught up by the obstacle. The creek itself had continued to gush over the root, eroding the creek bed on the opposite side, resulting in a waterfall with a drop of several feet. If he could get past that root, Ned thought, it would put a decent barrier between himself and whatever the tripod was firing at him, if only temporarily.

Lashing at the reins, Ned directed his horse down the bank and over the lip of the waterfall. The beast's hooves scrabbled for purchase in the mud, fetlocks surging against the water. Just a few feet more, Ned thought desperately, and—

There was another whoosh, and the creek *boiled*. With a shriek of agony the horse reared, slipped, and flew out over the lip of the now-steaming waterfall. The world spun as Ned left the saddle, throwing out his hands to ward off the inevitable impact. The last thing he heard before the creek bank rushed up to meet him was his horse screaming in pain, the sound abruptly cut off by the snap of its neck breaking as it slammed into the ground.

There was an indeterminable period of darkness. Eventually, though, the grey light of awareness crept over Ned. He was lying face down on the ground, his mouth clogged with moist clay. He raised his head, spat, and winced. His chest felt sore. *Must've bruised some ribs when I fell—*

Memory returned in a sudden rush. Adrenalin flooded Ned's veins, banishing the pain. Slowly he began to get up, then paused, before lowering himself back into the soil. Why was he still alive? Had the tripod given up? Had he somehow managed to lose it after the fall? The damned thing had seemed hell-bent upon destroying him, so why could he not hear any sounds of pursuit, or of the thing searching for him? Perhaps an unconscious target was no sport.

Or perhaps—and Ned's veins seemed to fill with ice at the thought—the thing was silently standing over him, waiting for him to rise.

Ned lay still and listened.

Nothing. There was only the slow stir of bushland in the wind, a few birds calling—

CHINK!

The ring of metal against metal sent a shiver down Ned's back. It seemed to be coming from somewhere very close. He waited.

CHINK! CHINK!

Slowly, carefully, Ned pushed himself up from the mud, and began to roll over on to his back.

The first thing he saw was his horse lying on the bank just a few feet away, its head twisted at an impossible angle. The lower parts of the beast's legs were white, hairless and steaming—cooked by the boiling creek water. Ned swallowed away the bile that rose in his throat and kept rolling, until he lay looking up at the lip of the waterfall, several feet above his head.

There was no sign of the tripod.

Grasping at exposed roots to assist himself, Ned clambered painfully to his feet and glanced around.

Maybe the infernal thing had moved on.

CHINK! CLICK!

The sound was coming from somewhere further back along the creek. Ned slowly crept up the bank, off to the side of the waterfall, then stretched up on the tips of his toes, peered over the top of the tree root—

—and found himself staring directly into one of the tripod's eyes, no more than a couple of yards away.

Ned stumbled backwards with a hoarse shout, tripping, falling back into the mud where he lay still, too terrified to move.

Nothing happened.

After nearly a minute, Ned got to his feet and cautiously peered over the top of the root again. A few moments of regarding the scene beyond made it clear to him what had occurred. The tripod, obviously believing the creek bed to be firm enough to take its weight, had attempted to cross the creek in pursuit of Ned. With its two back legs braced against the bank, the middle leg had slammed down into the middle of the creek and been instantly submerged in a deep sinkhole, vanishing almost all the way up to the hood. The entire mechanism had then toppled forward like a slain Goliath, and now lay stretched out in the middle of the creek, motionless and half-covered by clay and flowing water.

Ned quickly heaved himself up over the waterfall, and hesitantly approached the fallen giant. The mud beneath the tripod's hood burbled violently for a moment, and the entire machine slid a few feet closer to the sinkhole, pulled by the force of the sucking clay and weight of the vanished leg.

Dead, Ned thought triumphantly. Or, at the very least, securely trapped in the mud. It would take a team of oxen at least to pull the thing free; otherwise, in time, the entire mechanism would vanish forever.

CHINK!

Something terrible crawled up from underneath the opposite side of the hood, and glared at Ned with huge, black eyes.

"*God!*" Ned stumbled back several paces and fell again, then scrambled back to his feet, staring goggle-eyed at—

The thing was an abomination; a great, rounded bulk, heaving convulsively, fully the size of a drayhorse. Grey-brown skin glistened like wet leather in the sun. Beneath malevolent eyes, a lipless beak of a mouth quivered and panted and drooled. A dozen thin tentacles writhed beneath the mouth, clinging to the hood of the tripod, squirming like a nest of maddened snakes.

For a moment, Ned and the creature regarded each other without moving—Ned staring in disbelief, paralysed with shock and fear; the creature peering back, an expression of what Ned interpreted as cold calculation in its eyes.

Then, abruptly, the thing made a hideous gurgling sound, held up a shiny metallic object in one of its tentacles, and surged forwards, slithering down the side of the tripod's hood into the water and scuttling toward Ned like some enormous spider.

At that, Ned's paralysis broke. Almost automatically, both hands dropped to his belt to grab the butt of each Colt—both thankfully still there after his fall—which he swiftly drew and, without really bothering to aim, fired at the creature.

There was a moment of silence following the report. Ned blinked, smoke from the shots stinging his eyes, and for one horrible moment he wondered if the monster had proven as invulnerable to gunfire as the mechanism it had crawled from, and was even now closing the distance between them.

Then the smoke cleared, and Ned saw that his aim had been both true and effective. The creature lay twitching on the creek bed, green ichor spilling from a ragged hole in its side and dribbling away into the water. The object the creature had been brandishing lay beside it in the mud. Ned warily stepped forward and prodded it with the tip of his boot.

The gizmo was made from the same metal as the tripod and the cylinder, and despite its unfamiliar design it had a very functional look. Ned knew a tool when he saw one. But animals didn't use tools. Did demons or monsters? Ned glanced toward the fallen tripod. This creature—undoubtedly the controlling mind behind the actions of that infernal mechanism—must have been attempting to perform repairs of some sort, maybe even attempting to extricate its fallen mount. What in the name of blazes *was* this ungodly thing?

The creature gurgled, a couple of tentacles scrabbling weakly at Ned's boots. Disgusted, Ned raised his foot and ground the tentacles under his heel. The creature moaned painfully, green-flecked drool foaming at the corners of its mouth.

For a moment Ned almost felt sorry for the thing. Then he saw the look in the creature's eye—an awful gleam of malign intelligence. Even now, on the verge of death, the tentacles twitched weakly, the beast attempting to gather the strength to rise and destroy its enemy.

Ned leaned over the thing and drew back the hammer on one of his Colts. "Not so tough outside of a hood of metal, are ya?" he sneered coldly.

The creature gave a final squeal, full of desperation and hatred.

A single shot rang out, echoing briefly across the bush before fading to silence.

"Well, Ned?" Steve turned and gave Ned an unreadable look. "Where's this metal giant of yours?"

Ned swung down from behind Dan, off the horse, and looked around. This was definitely the place. "There's my horse," he said, nodding towards the unfortunate creature, "but…"

Where in blue blazes was the tripod? Surely it couldn't have been sucked into the sinkhole already?

Ned stared down into the creek. The mud at the water's edge bubbled scornfully at him.

"It's down there," he said heavily. "Two hours' walk back to the hut, half an hour to get back here with you…plenty of time to…" He wrung his hands together frustratedly. "*Blast it!*"

Dan muttered something under his breath.

"What?" snapped Ned, turning to face his brother.

"Nothin'."

Ned glared at Dan. "Spit it out."

Dan looked at the others for support, but they averted their eyes. "It's just…for something the size you told us about, it disappeared pretty quick…"

"You callin' me a liar, Dan?" Ned's tone was dangerously calm.

"So what about the *other* creature, Ned?" asked Steve. "The one that came out o' the machine?"

Ned gestured helplessly. A few feet away, a gelid, green stain fouled the mud. No monster. Just a couple of magpies screeching and fighting over a few remaining shreds of drying flesh.

"*Bastards!*" he roared. The birds took flight, squawking indignantly. Ned tore at his hair with both hands. Then, remembering: "The capsule!" He jumped up onto the horse behind his brother, reached past Dan's arms to grab the reins, and gave the mount a kick. The horse took off, leaving the others to catch up.

Minutes later Ned reached the crater, reined the horse to a halt and peered down into the pit. His face fell.

Joe rode up beside him. "Ned?" he asked, softly, although he could see for himself what was in the pit.

Dark, muddy water. Nothing more.

"Ned?"

Ned turned to Joe, his eyes pleading. "I'm not crazy, Joe—I *saw* it! The damned thing tried to—" He broke off, turning back to stare into the pit. "It *happened*!"

Joe nodded thoughtfully. "*Something* happened, Ned. Can't deny that." He nodded toward the pit. "Edge of that pit's all churned up. Freshly turned soil. And those burn-marks on the trees back there…" He shrugged. "But listen, Ned—if Dan or Steve or me came stumbling into camp with a story like the one you're telling, would you believe *us*?"

Ned bowed his head.

Joe chewed his lip for a moment. "*I* believe you, though." Ned looked up, startled.

Joe inclined his head. "It's a mad story, Ned—so mad, I couldn't see you making it up. Besides, there's blokes in England, scientists, who reckon there could be things like you said on Mars, and such. Maybe...I don't know—maybe this thing came here to find out how much of a fight we could put up if they decided to move in." He glanced over Ned's shoulder at Dan and Steve, then lowered his voice. "Can't see the others swallowing that, though. So maybe, in the interests of keeping this gang together, I reckon we might just say the troopers were shelling the area, and you and your horse copped one. Shook up your brains. I know it's tough, Ned, but...what d'ye reckon?"

Ned nodded slowly, and Joe thought that he'd never before seen the great man look so small and hollow.

"Armour!" said Ned suddenly. He sat up in the saddle, rough hands gripping Dan's shoulders tightly.

Dan craned his head around. "What's that?"

Ned didn't respond. *That creature was so easy to kill in the end,* he thought. *Just flesh and blood like the rest of us. But inside its infernal machine, safe behind a shell of armour—*

"Joe?"

Joe moved his horse in beside Dan's. "What's up, Ned?"

Ned paused for a moment, chewing his lip. "Those knights, back hundreds of years..."

Joe looked at him askance. "Knights? Yeah?"

"That armour they wore. D'ya reckon it would've stopped a bullet?"

"No guns back then, Ned." Joe flashed a smile. "What're you thinking?"

"Well, just that…" Ned hesitated again. "If we could get our hands on some solid pieces of metal—ploughshares, or some such…"

Joe nodded. "I think I see where you're going with this." He considered for a moment. "Maybe?"

"I can work with maybe."

Joe nodded. "I been thinking, Ned. Like I said, I believe you about…all that stuff you said." He ignored Dan's sniff of disbelief. "I reckon that tripod thing is gone forever. But that cylinder you mentioned…"

"What about it?"

"Well, the end of that furrow, the crater—that wasn't a sinkhole. It's just a big trench that's filled up with water. With some help, we could probably bail that pit dry. Or at least empty it sufficiently to be able to pull the cylinder up and out."

"I suppose," Ned allowed. "But what's the point? Other than to prove my tale?"

"Reason enough, ain't it?" Dan asked, and Steve snorted in amusement.

"No," Joe said sharply, and everyone turned to look at him. "I'm thinking…well, for starters, there's that metal it's made of. Probably the same stuff the tripod was made of, you said. Repels gunfire. No reason we couldn't use that in some way. Maybe even to make us some armour. Or at the very least sell it. But also, there's that weapon you mentioned."

"The heat gun."

"Yeah. The heat gun."

"Lost in the clay with the tripod, I reckon," Ned admitted.

"Yeah, but Ned—do you ever go out roaming without both of your Colts in your belt?"

Dan frowned. "What the hell are you talkin' about, Joe?"

"Well, I'm just thinking. You or I wouldn't head out into enemy territory without an extra gun, or extra ammunition, or the like, would we? So why wouldn't something coming here from another planet bring extra supplies with it? Spare parts, in case something happened to its tripod. Extra tools. Maybe even extra heat guns…"

There was a long silence.

"The cylinder," Ned said eventually.

"The cylinder," Joe confirmed.

Ned thought about it. If he could drum up a group of supporters in Oxley to help drain the furrow, utilise that metal, maybe find more of those amazing weapons…

Well, the Queen's army itself wouldn't be able to stand against the Kelly Gang! And from there—untold wealth? Power? A land swept clean of enemy forces?

That would make me a King! Ned thought. *No—a President!*

"Ned? What are you thinking?"

Ned turned and regarded Joe seriously for a moment. Then he grinned. "Just mulling over some plans for the future, Joe."

"Is that right?"

Ned nodded firmly. "Mark my words, Joe," he said, eyes shining brightly, "we're going to change history. Us, and whoever else decides to ride alongside—we're going to change *history!*"

Marlowe Strawl

**The Astounding Autobiographical Adventures of
Doctor Marlowe Daniel Jenkins Strawl Jr.
Gentleman Time-Traveller**

Chapter 1

*(In which our Narrator travels back in time to execute his wicked
Grandfather in the week just prior to the conception of the Narrator's
Father)*

...

Catflap

"I've got two words for you," Fletch said. "Cat. Analogues." He sat back in his chair, casually holding the lapels of his expensive jacket and grinning, as if that explained everything.

The Vork Diplomatic Consul nodded wisely and activated its cerebral netlink, initiating a low-level identiscan of the human sitting on the opposite side of the desk. The results of the scan scrolled across the Consul's ocular monitor almost immediately. It made interesting reading:

Aaron Edgar Fletcher, aka 'Fletch,' aka 'Edgar Aaronson,' aka 'Aaron Smith.' Human. Australian. Age: 42 (Earth years). Outstanding warrants issued by Australian Federal Police on numerous charges, including Fraud, Obtaining Monies by Deception, and Failure to Pay Debts.

There was also a fairly long list of Fletcher's various unsuccessful investment schemes. And an even longer list of extremely unhappy investors and creditors.

So—a confidence trickster, the Consul thought. *Or, at best, a businessman with a very poor grasp of ethics and, well, business.* But the Consul had no interest in crimes committed by extraterrestrials outside of the Vork Homeworld, and there was no record of anything that automatically warranted expulsion from the Vork Homeworld, Vork, such as violence or political subversion. And anyway, it had been a very slow day for the Consul. Perhaps hearing out this 'business proposition' would at least provide an amusing distraction.

"Cat analogues," the Consul repeated, then paused while its netlink advised it on the most diplomatic reaction. "Do go on."

"Okay, let me explain what I've got in mind," Fletch said.

"Please."

Fletch leaned forward and gazed earnestly into several of the Consul's eyes. "I," he began grandly, "am an entrepreneur."

The Consul nodded again, feeling that 'entrepreneur' was probably the nicest thing Aaron Fletcher had ever been called in his life.

"My…gift," Fletch continued, making a faux-humble gesture, "is that *I* see lucrative markets where others only see *stuff*. And with that vision comes a sort of instinctive knowledge of how to exploit those markets to their fullest—possible—potential!" He punctuated each word by tapping a finger on the Consul's desk.

The Consul resisted the urge to interject and ask how much profit Fletch's 'gift' had previously generated; partly because it already knew the answer (none), but mainly because Fletch's slightly over-the-top performance struck the Consul as being very funny indeed, and funny was an all too rare occurrence in the Consul's usual day to day. Instead of laughing, however, it fell back upon its diplomatic skills and uttered an almost imperceptibly sarcastic, "Gosh!"

"Gosh indeed! And, if you'd not guessed already, I reckon I've spotted an amazing, can't-fail, hugely profitable, untapped market right here on the Vork Homeworld!" Fletch's eyes glittered excitedly as he spoke and, despite itself, the Consul felt a slight thrill. Maybe *that* was Fletch's real talent, it thought: his ability to radiate an almost contagious sense of enthusiasm, which would excite potential investors, who thereafter became victims. And that, in the Consul's mind, raised Aaron Fletcher from being an amusing distraction to being an unamusing potential threat.

"I see," the Consul said brusquely, then leaned forward across the desk, deliberately displaying razor-sharp mandibles in a cold grin. "Well, why don't you tell me about this market you've found?"

Fletch shrank back in his chair. It wasn't just that the Consul looked like a three-metre tall funnel-web spider with far too many teeth, legs and eyes. It wasn't just that the Consul's grin looked like the last thing a shark victim sees. It was that, with the Consul suddenly all up in his face, Fletch was just now recalling that the Vork had a reputation that generally wasn't discussed in polite society, which was of the Vork being a highly intelligent race that greatly valued both science and the arts, yet which had a penchant for brutally enslaving other inhabited worlds. During the forty-odd years since first contact with Humanity, the Vork—who openly admitted that slavery was one of the less pleasant cornerstones of their civilisation, but what could you do?— had enslaved at least three other sentient races. The fact that their slave planets were essentially treated as larders was something that the Vork didn't address quite as openly, and Humanity—not wishing to upset amiable if tense diplomatic relations with the Vork—generally took the hint to do likewise, despite the unspoken understanding by all concerned that, given the opportunity, the Vork wouldn't hesitate to add Earth to their collection of slave worlds.

"Um…well, firstly, do you know what a cat is?"

The netlink offered nothing. "I do not," the Consul admitted.

Fletch leaned forward again. "A cat is a small domesticated Earthly mammal, considered by many humans as a desirable companion animal. They're pleasant to touch and hold, generally have an agreeable disposition, and express deep affection for their human owners while maintaining a high degree of independence."

"A pet, in other words."

"Oh, sorry. I wasn't sure you'd be aware of the concept. No offence intended."

"None taken," the Consul said, idly cleaning a fang with its feeding palps. "We have pets. Although they generally also serve as in-home livestock. Are these cats considered food animals?"

"Not…usually," Fletch replied carefully.

"I see. And what do cats have to do with this untapped market you claim to have spotted?"

"Ah, well, I'm just coming to that," Fletch said, beginning to sound more confident again. "See, despite their popularity, the issue with cats is that humans have become too used to them. They've been with us since the birth of human civilisation—"

The Consul coughed, disguising a snort of amusement.

"—and they're so commonplace and plentiful that you can breed and interbreed them at home, on the cheap. There's no real direct *profit* in cats anymore, despite more than fifty percent of humans owning at least one, other than through selling pet accessories and purebred strains. And, after so many centuries of physiological tampering, the genetic codes of many of the 'pure' breeds of cat are beginning to unravel, with entire strains becoming extinct." Fletch paused, waiting for the Consul to prompt him to continue.

The Consul remained silent, radiating polite impatience.

Fletch made a placating gesture. "Stay with me on this. See, I've realised that other planets must be home to species *analogous* to cats— animals to which the local sentients respond as humans do to cats, and which maybe even humans will respond to in the same way. I mean, you've mentioned that the Vork do keep pets. So I believe there's a totally untapped market for an animal like that, and whoever taps into it first stands to make an absolute fortune!"

The Consul held up a claw. "Okay, I think I can see where this is going. And it's an interesting pitch but, unfortunately, a completely impractical one."

"Look, I understand that—"

"No, wait a moment. Let me lay out some of the obvious obstacles, just off the top of my head, so we don't waste one another's time. For a start, there's Earth's own stance on importing organisms from Vork, due to so many of our indigenous species being utterly deadly to *your* indigenous species."

Including the Vork themselves, Fletch reflected. Which was why Earth had one simple policy with regards to allowing the Vork to visit Earth, even on a diplomatic basis: DON'T. In fact, this politely but firmly enforced exclusionary policy extended to cover all things produced or spawned on the Vork Homeworld—technology, artwork, flora, fauna—*everything*. There was even an embargo on sharing information about certain aspects of human existence with the Vork, lest that information be exploited.

"That's true," Fletch allowed. "But money motivates, y'know? Maybe this is the pitch that will open Earth's borders to the Vork."

The Consul smiled patronisingly. "A lovely notion. And I'm sure human avarice could open a great many doors." It paused, giving Fletch a pointed look. "But that brings me to a second obstacle, which is that the Vork—not unreasonably, I hope you'll agree—also have certain restrictions in place regarding Humanity. We've certainly shared information regarding our social structuring and artistic leanings, but— and do please excuse my bluntness—we very deliberately don't share information about our sciences, military capabilities, or biology, and for largely the same reasons Humanity doesn't share information with us."

Which was, both the Consul and Fletch knew, because both species were equally determined to come out on top of their mutual and constant covert power play, their seemingly-benign co-existence maintained only by the inability of each to compromise the security of the other.

Fletch smiled ingratiatingly. "So maybe Vork gets to be the bigger person in this situation, figuratively speaking. I mean, you already allow humans to visit Vork, which shows greater compromise than Earth has shown your people."

The Consul smiled politely. *It's not a compromise, you twat. We're not worried about humans running amok through the local population. Soft little pink things versus big spiky killing machines? Don't make me laugh.* "I'm sure you understand that this would absolutely have to be a mutual thing, Mister Fletcher. And I can't see Humanity making any concessions on this."

"I suspect you underestimate my species' love of profit."

I suspect I don't, the Consul thought. "You think the promise of profit would be sufficient to effect a policy change of this magnitude?"

Fletch steepled his fingers together. "No," he said carefully. "But I do think that some big payments to the right people—"

"I'd caution you to stop right there. While the Vork Empire certainly isn't averse to profitable enterprises, there are certain things I can guarantee we absolutely wouldn't do even if we were interested in your proposal, simply because they'd invite major conflict between your people and mine. There's a very solid reason we view slaves as livestock but absolutely reject the notion of treating human visitors to the Vork Homeworld as anything other than honoured guests. Other practices that the relevant Vork officials would—" the Consul consulted its netlink, "—*frown upon?*—would frown upon include bribery and, as I'm sure you were about to suggest, smuggling. So if—and it's clearly a huge and hypothetical 'if'—any form of payment was involved in the scheme you're suggesting, it would have to be completely above board, covering such things as shipping, import taxes, and security for your cat analogues and those supervising the transfer of the animals, including security for any Vork travelling to Earth."

Fletch blinked. "Security? For you guys?"

The Consul shrugged. "I mean, when you consider it'd be just a few of us amongst twelve billion humans... Let's be honest: your species does have a rather aggressive attitude towards anything that poses a potential threat. Nuke first, ask questions later."

"I'm...sure we wouldn't consider a few Vork visitors a threat. Not if there was such a massive trade deal at stake."

"Oh, don't be silly. Of *course* you would. Don't be bashful about it. The Vork and Humanity are both dangerously aggressive in their own, special ways. It's an evolutionary imperative. I mean, we'd certainly be assigning security to *you* if we were to let you go traipsing around outside of the Embassy, looking for your cat analogues."

"Really? You'd consider me that much of a potential threat?"

"Oh, not physically. That's a laughable notion. But there's always the possibility you could compromise our security. Assuming some peckish citizen didn't mistake you for a slave the second you stepped out onto the street, that is." The Consul smiled broadly, savouring Fletch's obvious discomfort. "But, getting back to the point at hand,

Earth would never allow members of our race to go planetside anyway. That's been made perfectly clear. And even if we were to, ah, *wave a magic wand* and wish away the obstacles I've already mentioned, there's one that would still undermine the whole venture in terms of getting any support for it whatsoever."

"Which is?"

"Well, there's no guarantee there are even any cat analogues *on* Vork. Or anywhere else in this wide old universe. It's an unsupported theory of yours, if you'll pardon my bluntness. So," the Consul shrugged apologetically, "with that said, I really do feel bad about wasting your time like this," *and mine*, it thought, "but—"

"But I've *seen* them!" Fletch interrupted, jumping to his feet.

The Consul sighed, surreptitiously reaching beneath the desk, a claw hovering just above the security alarm. Not that the Consul couldn't have slung Fletch out of the embassy all by itself, but the unions insisted that slinging was a job for security staff, and one didn't mess with the unions. Not on Vork. "Seen what?" it asked wearily.

"Cat analogues! I've already found them here!"

"Of *course* you have," the Consul said soothingly, pressing the button. Behind Fletch, the office door slid open to reveal two huge Vork security guards standing at the ready.

"I have!" Fletch insisted. "At the spaceport, just outside the secure area for offworlders, there was a Vork begging for money through the security fencing, and it was cradling some sort of big grub—"

"Grub?" the Consul interjected sharply.

"Yeah, a big white grub. About the size of an Earthly watermelon. Fat, lots of little white legs, big toothless mouth, lots of big brown eyes, and it was looking at me, and making this purring sound—*'roop-roop'*—like that, which is a super catlike thing, and it was so damned cute that I sort of felt compelled to reach through the fencing and stroke it and, when I did, the thing rolled its eyes and nuzzled up against my hand—"

"You're lucky you didn't lose that hand to the beggar," the Consul noted.

"In hindsight, yeah. But like I said, I just couldn't help myself. The way the grub behaved just hit all the right spots, psychologically speaking. And that's a very catlike behaviour too. Earthly cats actually domesticated *themselves* at least twice during our history, largely just by being cute so we wouldn't kick them out of our homes. They even learned to make a particular call solely around humans, mimicking the sound of a human baby, in order to ingratiate themselves."

"And you've picked up the same—" the Consul consulted its netlink again, "—what? *Vibe?* From this grub you saw?"

"Exactly!"

The Consul shot the guards a pointed look and they retreated, clearly disappointed by the broken promise of violence. As the office door slid shut again, the Consul fixed Fletch with an encouraging smile. "Do go on."

Fletch shrugged. "I mean…the grub's definitely a cat analogue. And if it could make a jaded bastard like me go all mushy, imagine how profitable it'd be potentially having twelve billion human beings feeling the same way. So," he raised an eyebrow, "what d'you think?"

The Consul rubbed its palps together thoughtfully for a moment. "Judging from the size of the market you're citing, you'd be looking to sell these cat analogues primarily on Earth itself, I gather? Not the outer human colonies?"

"Absolutely. Far easier and less expensive to promote to and supply one big centralised market than hundreds of smaller remote ones."

"Indeed. But, putting aside the issues of Earth's exclusionist policy, and the threat of undermining diplomatic relations, etcetera, how would you propose to do that exactly? Let's not, um, *beat around the bush*, Mister Fletcher. You're a wanted man back home." The Consul took a moment to enjoy the look of panic that flashed across Fletch's face. "Our intelligence agencies are extremely thorough, so please don't insult me with denials. You know it, I know it, and the authorities on Earth know it, so the moment you returned to Earth, or even had your name flagged as being involved with any local import schemes, they'd swarm over you like politicians over a free lunch." The Consul hadn't needed to consult its netlink for that reference. Some aspects of life were universal.

Fletch smiled weakly.

"None of which is of any concern to the Vork government, of course," the Consul continued. "Frankly, we couldn't care less about what you get up to on Earth. But it does beg the question of how exactly you'd propose to import the, ah, grubs. I mean, let's, um, *be real* for a moment. There's absolutely no way you can magic away all the legal issues obstructing your scheme. It's not going to happen. And I'm deeply sceptical of the idea that a few bribes would allow you to get around the Vork exclusionist policy, even assuming the Vork would be willing to engage in—"

"Yes, yes, I *know*," Fletch interrupted, "but look, I've got it all worked out, okay? Just let me run the plan by you, and see what you think!"

The Consul fixed Fletch with a piercing stare. "Very well. But please do get to the point quickly." It folded its claws together on the desk in front of it.

Fletch cleared his throat. "Okay, sure, well I have this mate—"

The Consul performed a reasonable impression of raising an eyebrow. "Your reproductive partner is in on this?"

"What? No. In this context, 'mate' is slang for 'friend'."

The Consul sighed inwardly, and made a 'carry on' gesture.

"So this mate of mine owns a huge tract of land near Alice Springs in Central Australia, middle of nowhere, breeds camels—" Fletch waved his hand dismissively. "Not important, sorry. But he does also run a huge operation legally farming marijuana—that's a popular local narcotic—with kilometres of greenhouse domes spread across some of the most remote country on Earth, all protected by the best security tech and personnel that money can buy. Now, the thing is, my mate wasn't originally a legitimate operator—"

"I'm astounded."

"—and quite a bit of the seed money for his current venture came from some investors who still take a fair percentage of his profits, as he can't afford to pay off his debts outright, despite literally earning billions per annum."

"So you'd suggest a complete payoff to the creditors as a sort of bribe to your friend?"

Fletch held up a hand. "Well, yes, but that's only part of it."

"Proceed."

"So one of my mate's biggest markets is the Telstar orbiting spacedock." Fletch shrugged. "I assume there must be fuck-all else to do up there outside of working hours. Now, my mate does periodically supply marijuana to the customs officials on both Telstar and the local Earthside port in exchange for turning a blind eye to some of his other dealings—black-market offworld goods, stuff like that. They let it pass through without any scans, searches, or awkward questions."

The Consul nodded thoughtfully. "I see. So if a sizeable, unmarked shipment arrived on the Telstar addressed to your friend, he'd be able to take receipt with no awkward questions from any customs agents, and…what? Hide the goods on his property?"

"I mean, we'd need to label it as coming from somewhere other than Vork, with a forged data trail in case anyone with a sense of responsibility took it upon themselves to look a bit too closely at the packing slips, but yeah. And then he'd organise sale and distribution, using his own infrastructure and contacts."

The Consul drummed its claws against the desk. "I'm wondering just how feasible it would really be for such shipments to be continuous, rather than occasional, in order to be able to supply your friend with sufficient quantities of the grub to enable widespread distribution. A constant flow of shipments hugely increases the risk of discovery, regardless of how well you bribe the officials."

"I figured we'd make it just a couple of shipments, and then my mate could use the imported grubs as breeding stock."

The Consul shook its head. "It wouldn't work."

"Why not?"

The Consul hesitated for a moment. "Even on Vork, the grubs are difficult to breed in captivity."

Fletch nodded. "Okay. Well, in that case, cloning? My mate routinely uses reproductive technologies to produce seed and seedling stock. I assume he'd be open to repurposing some of his system to produce eggs or embryos instead of flora."

The Consul nodded slowly. "Yes. That could work."

"So…you're interested? Are you in?"

"Mmmm…interested, certainly," the Consul admitted. "But I'd like to hear about some of the finer details of the scheme before I commit to taking it to any potential local backers."

"No worries!" Fletch grinned, rubbing his hands together. "Okay, so we import the grubs, hide some away as cloning stock, introduce a few into a suitable local environment outside of the farm itself but still within my mate's property, then my mate files all the relevant paperwork to farm these critters he's 'discovered.' The local environmental bods will doubtless identify the grubs as being of extraterrestrial origin—which is fine, things like this do happen on Earth from time to time given that we have free trade with various other worlds, just so long as the grubs are found to be harmless—" He gave the Consul a look. "They *are* harmless, I gather?"

The Consul nodded. "Completely."

"Okay, great, so they run their tests, find the grubs harmless, and assume they were brought in by accident on the bottom of someone's shoe, or something. No reason to suspect they're from Vork, or to test for it, given they have no information on Vork biology, and no reason to suspect the original stock was bred on my mate's farm. A few bribes can take care of any suspicions on that front, anyway. So my mate's claim on them becomes legal." Fletch adopted a conspiratorial tone. "Maxwell's Clause. If you find a non-sentient alien organism on your property, and it's not harmful in any way, it's yours. Maxwell made a fortune out of Sirian glow-worms—"

"*Anyway...*" the Consul prompted.

"Sorry. Anyway, at this point we start up large scale ongoing cloning of the grubs, completely legally, and build up stock for—" Fletch paused. "Wait. Do these grubs—these…what d'you actually call 'em on Vork?"

The Consul hesitated again. "*Chuusa.*"

"Okay, *chuusa* grubs—"

"No, just *chuusa*. *Chuusa* literally means 'grub,' so calling them *chuusa* grubs would be calling them grub grubs."

Fletch held up his hands placatingly. "Okay, so how long do these *chuusa* actually live?"

"Roughly—" the Consul consulted its netlink, "—four Earthly years?"

"Okay, so let's assume that after about eighteen months we have, say, a hundred thousand *chuusa*. Maybe more or less, but we can work that out later. Now, at this point my mate starts selling and distributing the *chuusa* as pets. Exotic cat analogues. 'Be the first on your block,' etcetera. I'll be directing the whole operation from offworld, of course. Somewhere close, but with no extradition laws, just in case. Titan, maybe. Possibly Ganymede. I've always wanted to see—"

"Ahem."

"Sorry, getting ahead of myself. Anyway, we start off by selling the *chuusa* solely to the rich for a couple of years, to recover costs. Then we drop the price and start selling to the average income earner. Everyone'll want one, and if we maintain healthy stock levels we can meet that demand for as long as it lasts!" Fletch leaned back, grinning. "A plan with no flaws. And I'm anticipating sufficient revenue just within the first few months of sales to be able to make it worthwhile for all invested parties."

"That...all sounds very promising," the Consul admitted.

There was a long pause.

"Um..." Fletch said, eventually.

"Yes?"

"Well..." Fletch gave a slight shrug. "Don't...you want to know roughly *how* worthwhile this'll be for the Vork?"

"Oh." The Consul stared at Fletch for a moment, then smiled. "Yes. Yes, of course. Please."

"Right, then." Fletch pulled a slimline comm-cell from the inner pocket of his jacket and ran some calculations, then turned the screen around to show the Consul. "So we can sell each *chuusa* for at least five grand Australian initially—sorry, I'm not sure how that converts into local currency—"

"That's okay, go on."

"Okay, and then about half that when we drop the price for the plebs. So in a year, we make…" Fletch punched in some more calculations, and again displayed the results. "I figure my mate'll accept fifteen percent, maybe less since us paying off his creditors will allow him to make far more profit on his marijuana sales. Then there's my cut as operations manager—say, forty percent. And the remainder goes to your government, or whoever's organising things from Vork. Obviously most of the profits for the first year'll go on recouping the bribes and setup costs. But," more calculations, "*this* is what I estimate we'd be making, minimum, after the first year. And if the *chuusa* only have a four-year lifespan, we can assume the annual turnover will continue to grow as existing owners replace dead chuusa, and new buyers enter the market. So over the first five years *this* is, conservatively, what the Vork could be making out of this deal…" Fletch indicated the figure at the bottom of the screen.

The Consul noted the figure, then leaned slowly back in its seat.

Fletch waited, trying not to fidget nervously in his seat. "So?" he asked eventually.

The Consul regarded Fletch silently for a moment. Then it picked up a stylus from a caddy on the desktop, fished a piece of delicate parchment from a drawer, and began to scrawl something on it. After a moment it glanced up again, pushing the parchment over to Fletch. "The guards outside the door are monitoring our conversation, and I'm hereby instructing them to organise transport to take you straight to the Office of Commerce and Trade. When you arrive, show them that document and ask to see the Minister of Trade Relations immediately."

Fletch cautiously picked up the document. "What is it?"

"It's a letter of authority, signed by a duly appointed proxy for the Vork government—that's me—stating that we're hoping to enter into a contract with one Aaron Edgar Fletcher to assist in the exportation of *chuusa* to Earth. The Minister is further instructed to, um, *get the ball rolling* immediately regarding further discussion and refinement of the operation plan, and once all the details are hammered out—"

A huge grin spread across Fletch's face. "Really? Seriously?"

"Absolutely." The Consul extended a claw across the desk, and Fletch automatically clasped it. "I'll transmit a recording of our conversation to the Trade Relations office to assist with the process."

"Oh, that's fantastic!" Fletch sprang from his chair, vigorously shaking the Consul's claw. "*Thank* you!"

"You're very welcome, Mister Fletcher. Oh, and by the way...?"

"Yes?"

The Consul kept its smile pleasant. "As previously stated, we're genuinely unconcerned with your criminal record. *But*—" the smile vanished as the Consul leaned forward, slipping its claw from Fletch's grip, "—if you even *think* about trying to swindle the Vork in any way, shape, or form...we'll have you for breakfast."

The way the Consul said it, it didn't sound like a euphemism. Because it wasn't.

Fletch smiled nervously, placing a hand against his chest. "Oh, absolutely! I'd never dream of..." He trailed off. "Look, you can absolutely trust me, okay? No need for threats."

"The Vork don't make *threats*, Mister Fletcher. Only promises."

Fletch paled.

"Good day, Mister Fletcher." The Consul's warm smile returned. "It's been lovely doing business with you."

Fletch nodded hesitantly, then rose from his chair and left the Consul's office, clutching the document in his hand.

As soon as the door closed, the Consul opened a communication via its netlink. "Message to Security Central. Apparently we've got vagrants openly begging along the security fences at the spaceport in plain sight of visiting extraterrestrials—with *chuusa* in tow, no less! Can we please have that dealt with immediately?" It paused. "But be...*nice* about it." It tagged the communication as completed, then opened a new link to the Office of Commerce and Trade, sending through the recorded conversation with Fletch along with relevant notations. That done, the Consul sent through a request to the

Department of Offworld Incursion requesting a Priority One response to discuss an urgent matter. Then it called for a vehicle to take it home for the day, feeling it had earned an early mark.

The *chuusa* were milling around the entrance when the Consul arrived back at its burrow; the whole clutch gazing up at it, rubbing against its legs, purring expectantly. The Consul dutifully pulled a bag of kibble from its satchel and sprinkled a clawful at its feet, then stepped back and cooed as they scampered across the floor on tiny white legs, sucking up morsels into their wide, toothless mouths.

Such a wonderful period of innocence in their lives, the Consul thought. *Enjoy it while you can, little ones*. In just a few short years the *chuusa* would rapidly transmute into their ravenous adolescent forms, mindlessly consuming anything they could sink their razor-sharp teeth into to fuel their growth.

The Consul's eyes twinkled as it considered what a hundred thousand adolescents in the grip of growth fever could do to the human population of Earth.

And afterwards, there'll be an Earth-born occupation force of adult Vork...

It was just too perfect. After decades of failing to compromise Earth security protocols, the Vork Empire had—completely out of the blue—essentially been presented with access via the back door.

A catflap, the netlink whispered.

The Consul tilted its head to one side and regarded the *chuusa*. *Our beautiful children*, it thought contentedly. *They're going to make their parents so proud...*

Full Circle

"This is the tenth case this week." Doctor Hibbert crossed his arms and nodded towards the hunched figure on the opposite side of the one-way mirror. Oblivious to being watched, James' grandfather continued to scrawl on the far wall of the observation room, pausing occasionally to select different-coloured crayons from the box Hibbert had offered upon his arrival.

"Oh. So…is it not as bad as the media's making out, then? I thought—"

"I mean that it's the tenth case for me. And it's only Tuesday. And every single one of my colleagues, and all of their colleagues, are dealing with more cases every single day. We can definitely call it a global…I don't know. Pandemic? Phenomenon? Whatever it is, it's spreading exponentially."

James nodded wearily. "Any word of a cure, or…I dunno, a treatment, at least?"

"We don't even know what it *is* yet. There's no evidence of a virus or infection or anything of that nature, besides which the pattern of affliction doesn't support that idea, even if whatever-it-is was airborne.

And without identification, they can't even begin to formulate a treatment." The Doctor seemed about to say more, then hesitated.

"What?" James asked.

"Well…" Hibbert sighed. "Look, I do have a theory…"

"About treatment?"

"No, about what it is. But let me make this absolutely clear: it's not a diagnosis. It's literally just a personal theory, among a thousand different theories being offered right now."

James nodded. "Okay, sure, I understand. What's the theory?"

Hibbert hesitated again, then said, "Okay, look—your grandfather is just under two-hundred years old, correct?"

"One-hundred and ninety-seven, yeah."

"Right. So that puts him in the first generation of people to successfully receive one of the various longevity treatments at age thirteen to nineteen?"

"He was given the EwigJung shot, I think. In his mid-teens, maybe? I'd have to ask my mum."

Hibbert nodded. "I'd assume so. From what we've seen, the vast majority of those currently afflicted received their treatments during the first fifteen-odd years of those treatments being available through public health systems."

James stared at Hibbert. "So…what? This is caused by some issue with the early treatments?"

Hibbert shook his head. "No. At least, not directly, I don't think."

James furrowed his brow. "I don't understand. What are you trying to say?"

Hibbert uncrossed his arms. "Just stay with me on this. It's all relevant." He took a moment to collect his thoughts. "Are you aware that human beings are genetically programmed for only a thirty-year lifespan?"

"Yes, I've heard that. But we overcame that evolutionary use-by date with medicines and vaccines, and stuff like that, yeah?"

"Yes, that's true. And it's not so much that we're supposed to drop dead at thirty, just that that's the age where our bodies naturally start to go downhill. And in the environments in which our ancestors evolved, that degradation was usually sufficient to quickly remove them from the gene pool. So modern humans, being able to better control their bodies and environments, have also been able to increase their longevity, which is great. But with the more extreme extensions of age we've seen over the past few hundred years, we've also opened ourselves to conditions that would never develop if people died at thirty. We become more prone to various types of cancer, for example, as well as to Alzheimer's and Parkinson's, all of which either terminate the aging process, or simulate the *reversal* of aging by mimicking the conditions of infancy. And I think that this—" Hibbert nodded again towards the occupant of the observation room, "—may be a similar condition, although admittedly an astoundingly extreme one, finally unlocked now that we've made the jump from living until the age of ninety to living beyond the age of two hundred."

"So…what? It's a built-in genetic disorder, but one we're only seeing now because of the longevity treatments?"

Hibbert shrugged. "Maybe two-hundred odd years is the point at which the human body stops manifesting illnesses that *simulate* the reversal of aging, and actually *does* it."

"But…he *isn't* getting younger!"

"But there *has* been a regression. A very obvious physical one. Some sort of, I don't know…radical spontaneous mutation, as opposed to an actual illness? Maybe it's some sort of equivalent to reverting back to a physical age of thirty. Or maybe this…" Hibbert made a vague gesture, "this form represents a sort of bodily reboot, and your grandfather's physical age is immaterial. Maybe it's the mental regression that's important. I genuinely don't know. Again, it's all just a theory. I'm just attempting to make sense of this whole thing." He shrugged apologetically.

James considered this for a moment. "But *everyone* receives longevity treatments now! It's been part of universal healthcare for the past two-hundred years! So if you're correct, that would mean…"

Hibbert said nothing.

"Christ." James' face was pale.

"If I'm correct—and it *is* just an 'if'—then we've clearly set ourselves up for a massive fall. Humanity, I mean. The treatments have already hugely changed society over the past couple of centuries, with the old getting older while maintaining peak health, and thus remaining in the upper echelons of industry and power. Naturally, we stopped producing as many children in order to balance things out, which is why approximately eighty percent of the world population is now over the age of one-hundred and fifty, but..." Hibbert regarded James carefully. "Imagine what'll happen if eighty percent of people become afflicted with this thing over the next fifty years."

There was a long silence.

"But hopefully I'm wrong," Hibbert continued eventually, "and this thing will be sorted out before things get too chaotic."

James pressed his forehead against the one-way mirror. "Okay. So...what happens now, with *him*?"

"All you can do at this point is take your grandfather home," Hibbert said gently. "There'll undoubtedly be widespread notifications if there are any developments regarding treatment."

James stood up, nodding slowly. "Yeah, okay. Can I...?"

Hibbert nodded, and moved to open the door beside the mirror. "Please."

James took a hesitant step into the observation room. "Gramps?"

James' grandfather paused, an orange crayon gripped awkwardly in one hairy paw.

"Gramps? It's time to go..."

James' grandfather turned, staring blankly at his grandson from beneath a bony brow, lips curled back from his heavy jaw in an expression of frustration. He *knew* the words, could almost grasp the meaning behind them, but—

No. It was gone.

Grunting irritably, he turned back to the picture he'd been scrawling onto the wall; two rudimentary human figures standing on opposite sides of a crudely-drawn rectangle. He knew that others— many others—like himself would soon be coming to this strange, white cave, so he needed to finish the picture before sundown, before the predators came out, so the knowledge of what went on in this place could be passed along.

Alien Space Nazis Must Die!

He blinked, and found himself once again sitting in the shuttle cockpit. He jumped to his feet, then swayed as a wave of faintness and nausea swept over him. His guts heaved, but—

I don't even have a stomach...

And suddenly the full weight of reality crashed in upon him. He fell to the deck and lay there, convulsing. Dimly, he heard Kroll say: "So sorry. But better this way…"

Hidden inside the ventilation duct, Lars Janssen peered cautiously through the grille at the shuttle-bay beyond; or, more accurately, at the back of the trooper's head currently blocking his view of the shuttle-bay. The trooper, he noticed, had dandruff; greasy white flakes spilling out from beneath the Nazi's helmet, speckling the collar of his uniform. Lars shook his head reprovingly, then glanced at his watch. Only ten minutes before the explosives went off. If he wasn't off this KillMoon by then…

Lars pushed gently against the bottom of the grille, which swung silently outwards from the wall. He slid forward slightly to brace the back of his neck against the underside of the raised grille to prevent it from swinging shut again, then slowly reached out with both hands towards the back of the unsuspecting trooper's neck…

…paused…

Then lunged forward, grabbed, and *twisted*.

Snap!

Lars slid swiftly from his hiding-spot, catching the body as it fell and gently lowering it to the deck. He spared the dead trooper a brief glance—the reptilian yellow eyes already glazing—and smirked.

Galactic Master-Race? Not from where I'm standing…

Lars liberated the pulse-rifle from the trooper's death-grip, hefting it with practiced ease, and scanned the bay cautiously. Darkness and silence. Aside from a couple of shuttles parked nearby, dimly visible in the gloom, the area seemed utterly deserted. Lars moved towards the nearest craft.

He'd taken barely three steps before he heard a sound that stopped him in his tracks: a sudden low hum that escalated quickly into the higher octaves before accelerating to a pitch inaudible to the human ear.

Hummmmmm…

It was the sound of a pulse-rifle being primed to fire.

Lars stopped in his tracks, finger tightening against the trigger of his weapon. This was bad, but he was nonetheless confident in his own speedy reflexes, so if he could just work out where the other guy was standing—

Hummmmmm…

Hummmmmm…

Humm-Humm-Humm-Hummity-Humm-Humm-de-Humm…

Dammit!

Apparently the other guy was standing all around him.

Abruptly, the lights flicked on to reveal a squad of Nazi troopers surrounding Lars, each aiming his rifle unwaveringly at the agent's head. Lars sighed theatrically and raised his hands in surrender. An officer stepped forward and curtly removed the rifle from Lars' grasp. Lars beamed disarmingly. "So…somebody order a candygram?"

"Flippant as ever, Janssen." The mob parted, and a depressingly familiar figure walked forward through the resulting gap.

"Well, well." Lars nodded. "Reichsführer Hottschtepper. I didn't think I'd be seeing *you* again. Last time we met, you wound up on the receiving end of a napalm enema. You must be using a very effective brand of haemorrhoid cream."

Hottschtepper smiled horribly, grey lips peeling back to display a dentist's nightmare of sharklike teeth. "Did you really think you could infiltrate zis KillMoon undetected?"

"Frankly, yes. Mind if I put my hands down?"

Hottschtepper regarded him coolly. "*Ja.* But keep them vere I can see them."

Lars nodded amiably as he lowered his arms. "Sooo…what happens now?"

Hottschtepper smirked. "Now? *You die!* Squad! Prepare to carry out execution!" He sighed as his troopers snapped into position. "Oh— and those of you standing behind ze prisoner? Will you *please* move around to stand with ze others, in case Janssen ducks? That's how he got avay last time." He stepped quickly out of the line of fire as the troopers repositioned themselves. "Squad ready? Aim—!"

"Um!" Lars raised his hand. "Mind if I blow my nose first?"

Hottschtepper regarded him incredulously. "Ve are about to *shoot* you! Does it truly matter that you die with a nose full of bogies?"

"Sorry," Lars apologised, "it's just that…oh, I'm going to sneeze! Ah! Ah! *Ahhhh—!*" he cupped a hand over his nose, "*—CHOO!*" Unseen by Lars' captors, the tiny grenade hidden up his right nostril flew out into his palm. Lars made a show of wiping his nose with the back of his hand, using the motion to surreptitiously affix the grenade to the nail of his right index finger.

"Are you quite done?" Hottschtepper enquired, with mock-sweetness.

"Yep, all done, thanks!"

"Are you *quite* sure? Vould you perhaps like me to fetch you a Kleenex?"

Lars waved away the offer. "No, all good, thanks. You're good to go."

Hottschtepper rolled his eyes. "*Wunderbar!* So! Squad ready? Aim—!"

"Say cheese!" Lars shut his eyes tightly and flicked his index finger in the direction of the assembled troopers, the grenade shooting through the air to hit the deck in front of the firing squad, where it exploded in a searing flash of light. The entire squad staggered back, flashblinded. Lars leapt forward and tore a pulse-rifle from the grip of the nearest trooper, immediately thumbing the weapon to auto and strafing the squad with plasma-fire. Within seconds Lars was the last man standing—apart from Hottschtepper, who was stumbling blindly towards the exit. "Oh no you don't!" Lars sprinted after the fleeing Nazi, catching up to him within moments, grabbing his shoulder and spinning him around before delivering a cracking blow to his jaw. "*That's* for all the innocents and agents who've died at your hands!" Lars snarled. "And *this*—" a second blow laid the Nazi out cold, "—is for *me!*"

Pausing only to catch his breath, Lars glanced at his watch. Barely a minute left! He sprinted towards the nearest shuttle, charged up the ramp, scrambled into the cockpit and threw himself into the pilot's chair, hands flickering across the flight console. *Closing the ramp! Priming the drive! Ignition!* With a piercing whine the craft shot forwards, punctured the containment field, and flew out into open space. Lars waited until he judged the shuttle was out of range of the KillMoon's anti-spacecraft batteries, then leaned forward and activated the comm. "Hello, KillMoon switchboard? Priority call for Reichsführer Hottschtepper…"

There was a slight pause. Then: "*Ja?*"

"Hottschtepper?"

"Janssen?? Zere is no escape! In moments ze DeathWaffen will be on your trail! And then…*you will meet your doom!*"

"I'm afraid not, Hottschtepper. You see, I've left a little gift for you under your KillMoon's primary reactor." Lars regarded his watch. "And you've got…ten seconds left in which to thank me!"

"*VHAT??*"

Lars' expression hardened. "Goodbye, Reichsführer!"

"I vill see you in *HECK*, Janssen! *IN HECK!!*"

The comm went dead as a silent flash briefly lit up the endless night of space.

Lars sighed. Mission accomplished. Time to head back to Central Headquarters, debrief, and prepare for the next assignment. No rest for the heroic. An agent's job was never done. So long as the Alien Space Nazis remained a threat to Intergalactic freedom, there would always be another operation, another counterstrike, another assassination to undertake.

Sometimes, Lars thought, it seemed like he'd been doing this job forever…

"Greeting?"

Lars blinked, then regarded the comm with a frown. "Hello? Who's that?"

"Greeting?"

"Identify yourself, please."

A clattering gargle emanated from the comm, Lars identifying two distinct voices—if indeed it was speech he was hearing, as opposed to a couple of somebodies or some*things* clearing their throats—that he had the distinct impression were addressing one another rather than himself. After a moment, a voice different to the one that had suggested greeting spoke.

"Am Kroll, Commander of Nine Hundred and Twelfth Spawning of Eighteenth Fleet of Elevated Tertiary Hive of Hoosh of Seventeenth Broodworld of Forty Second Quadrant of Fifteenth Outreach of Generation Ark Fleet of Twelfth Great Diaspora of Year of Golden Fettling of Second Glorious Arthrod Empire!"

"Gosh. *That*…is certainly an impressive address. It must make mailing out Christmas cards very time-consuming."

There was a slight pause, then: "What?"

Lars waved a hand dismissively, despite knowing the gesture would go unseen. "Sorry. Agency humour. We have it drummed into us in basic training."

Another pause. "Er...to whom I speak?" Kroll asked eventually.

"This is Lars Janssen of the Intergalactic Anti Alien Space Nazi Agency. State your business, Commander."

More gargling and clattering.

"I *can* still hear you, you know," Lars interrupted wearily.

There was a distinctly embarrassed pause.

Kroll cleared his (?) throat and addressed Lars again. "Believe yourself to be Lars Janssen of Intergalactic Anti Alien Space Nazi Agency? Fight Alien Space Nazis? Fight to free galaxy?"

Lars glanced around the cockpit, then raised an eyebrow and regarded the comm again. "I mean...that's what it says on my onboarding paperwork, yes."

Kroll made an odd rattling sound. "Apologies. No easy way to tell, but...you *not* Lars Janssen."

"I'm not?"

"Not."

Lars smiled thinly. "*Okaaaaaaay*—so, who am I?"

"Not know. But not Lars Janssen. Not agent of IAASNA. Not fight Alien Space Nazis. Not even sit in shuttle right now, talking to us."

"Riiiiiiiiight. So where do *you* think I am right now, then?"

"Body connect to 'Ultra-Immersive Entertainment System.' Program running on system is titled 'Alien Space Nazis Must Die!'."

Lars smiled dismissively. "So you're saying I'm...what? Playing some sort of immersive game?"

"Yes. You play *character* named Lars Janssen. We currently observe your gameplay on monitor."

Lars sighed. "Right. Yeah. Sure. Okay. Listen, Commander Kroll, I don't know what you've been smoking, but—"

"We observe you for two cycles now," Kroll interrupted. "Get feel for game. Very...exaggerated. Unrealistic."

"You think my life is unrealistic? I'm...not quite sure how to take that, frankly."

"Not think your life too convenient?" Kroll pressed. "Prison always have hidden exit? Guard never shoot straight? Escape explosion with only seconds to spare? Is believable? Is even vaguely credible?"

"I mean—"

"No! Is not! Is fantasy world! Not real!"

"Go away, Kroll," Lars snapped. "Stop wasting my time!"

More gargling. Then the first voice, clearly a subordinate of Kroll's, said: "We find memory-suppressant installed in system, which clearly reason you not notice being inside a constructed reality. With Commander's permission, I deactivate this now. Just giving you warning."

"Oh, for Chrissake!" Lars leaned forward to switch off the comm, and—

"Deactivating…"

Light explodes around him. Above, a grossly swollen sun fills the sky. Below, the soil is ash. Deep underground, the sterile remnants of humanity slumber in a drug-induced stasis, bodies laid out on a seemingly endless number of metal gurneys, while artificial intelligences postulate a means to repopulate the Earth.

He dives deeper. Remembering…

The A.I.s are set to reawaken their wards when a viable solution to their fertility becomes apparent; meanwhile, in order to prevent psychosis due to sensory deprivation, the sleepers remain wired into state-of-the-art gaming modules, all knowledge of their reality suppressed to further cushion them against the weight of their situation. Thus, gamers may fight at the O.K. Corral or Gallipoli, and actually believe they are there. They can take Neil Armstrong's infamous step, or pilot the Enola Gay over Hiroshima, or step into the personas of a vast range of fictional characters.

Deeper…

He seems to float above himself, looking down at the senseless, emaciated figure huddled on the gurney, cocooned in a web of cannulas and tubes and wiring, a compact gamelink puncturing the top of his skull. A small metallic tag hanging from just above the puncture point reads:

**RealPlay Games
Alien Space Nazis Must Die!
A Lars Janssen Adventure**

He reaches out to touch the wire, and—

He blinked, and found himself once again sitting in the shuttle cockpit. He jumped to his feet, then swayed as a wave of faintness and nausea swept over him. His guts heaved, but—

I don't even have a stomach...

And suddenly the full weight of reality crashed in upon him. He fell to the deck and lay there, convulsing. Dimly, he heard Kroll say: "So sorry. But better this way…"

Later, glancing around the cockpit, he wondered how he could have thought all this was real. The surfaces were too perfect and angular, the colours too monotonous, the buttons and displays obviously mere pixelated representations. *But of course*, he told himself, *the software altered my perception sufficiently for me to accept it all without—*

"Questions?" Kroll asked, over the comm.

Reg Prescott rubbed his forehead, still feeling groggy. Random recollections of pre-game life kept popping into his head like scum floating to the top of a septic tank; a wholly disorienting and unpleasant experience. And there was something odd about his hands; something he couldn't quite put his finger on. "Dunno. Some of it's coming back. Although…" He glanced at the comm. "Are you guys actually, y'know… *aliens?* Or is that just something the game made up?"

"To you, yes, aliens. Last of Arthrod race."

"Last?"

Kroll sighed. "Millennia ago, fight war. Bioweapons induce genetic decay and sterility. Survivors flee in fleet of generation arks, seek new home. Scientists think Earth habitable, hope humanity sufficiently advanced to reverse our sterility. But solar flare hit before we arrive. Qandho make joke at our expense, yes?"

"Qandho?"

"Our faith. Qandho dictate sanctity of life above all else. For us, essential to both spiritual and physical survival. Arthrod once warrior race, governed by instincts not appropriate in enclosed environment of ark. So sublimate aggression by focus upon Qandho. Is ancient religion, long lapsed, but now considered vital to continued survival, and thus again stringently observed. Will teach you dictates of Qandho, once you sufficiently recovered."

Great, Reg thought. *Missionaries from outer space.* "Um…actually, I'm an atheist."

Kroll made a querying sound.

"Not religious. Don't believe in God. Or this…Qandho of yours."

"Blasphemy!" Kroll muttered.

"Look, I didn't mean to offend—"

"No, no, am sorry," Kroll apologised, still sounding pissed. "Spend life in company of faithful, is shock to meet infidel."

"Er, yeah…" Reg decided a change of topic was obviously in order. "Listen, perhaps we *can* solve your sterility problem. After all, if the A.I.s can sort out *our* situation, then…" He frowned. "Although…I guess they're *still* looking for a solution, aren't they? Otherwise they'd have woken us up. I don't s'pose it'll take much longer, though. The boffins said five years at the most."

There was a long, awkward pause.

"Hello?" Reg prompted.

"Er…"

"What?"

"No easy way to say," Kroll said slowly, "but—from information we glean from your systems—after you enter stasis, A.I.s realise cannot reverse sterility or other genetic damage from solar flare, and decide only option to preserve humanity is create androids into which human race-memory downloaded. But A.I.s realise preservation of memory alone not appeal to humanity, so decide to leave you in stasis. A.I.s and androids leave Earth to establish own civilisation elsewhere." He paused. "Stasis run on automatic ever since."

Reg took a moment to digest this. "So…how long have I…I mean, how long have all the survivors been stuck in stasis?"

"You play game now for sixty-three local solar cycles. Lucky we arrive. Otherwise…"

Reg's head swam. "It's not true—it can't be! You're lying!" He looked down at his hands; young and far too perfect. "Game!" he called out. "Change player avatar to reflect external image." His hands flickered, morphing to display the lines and liver spots of advanced age. Reg moaned softly.

Kroll was right. The A.I.s had failed.

Reg buried his face in his hands, feeling numb. "How many left?" he asked eventually. "Most of the other sleepers were older than me. How many survived?"

"Last count," Kroll's subordinate said hesitantly, "three thousand, six hundred, forty-two."

"WHAT?? But…there were over five million of us!"

The Arthrods remained silent.

"Right. Right. Well," Reg said, far too calmly, "it's not the end of the world. We've still got time to look at new avenues of research. Some of the other surviving sleepers would have gone in as children. Infants, even. Minimal genetic damage. And it's not like we need a viable breeding population—I mean, we can look at cloning, or—"

"So sorry," Kroll muttered.

"Oh, for Chrissake! What??"

"Flare activity increasing, not subsiding. Even your youngest now genetically damaged. And neither your cloning tech nor ours up to working around that."

Reg nodded slowly. So. He was going to die. *Everyone* was going to die. The thought left him feeling oddly detached. Too much to take in, he supposed. After almost a minute of silence, he asked: "So. What happens now?"

"Well, leave game," Kroll said. "Come with us."

Reg frowned. "Why?"

"Sorry?"

"I mean…why? You can't help us. We're dead whatever we do. And we can't help you, either. You were hoping we could solve your problems, remember?"

"Of course." Kroll sounded nonplussed. "Cannot save humanity. But extend remaining life by leaving Earth. Our fleet can accommodate all remaining humans…"

If you leave Earth, you leave the game…

An icy finger seemed to penetrate Reg's numbness. If he left the game, he left the comfort and familiarity of a fantasy world where he could *make a difference*, fighting the forces of evil; a place where his life actually meant something, even if it was a game-induced delusion. Reality, on the other hand, was a brutal nightmare offering only a bleak, short, ultimately futile existence before his entire species faded into extinction, lost forever in time and memory.

So…if that awful conclusion was inevitable, why take the hard way out?

"Listen," Reg said slowly, "I appreciate all you've done. I really do. But…I think maybe I'll just stay here."

There was a shocked silence.

"What??" Kroll demanded. "Cannot be serious! Life most valuable gift Qandho give! To stay in game, to deny reality and life, is…*blasphemous!*"

Reg blew out his cheeks, glancing listlessly around the cockpit. "Well…" he shrugged apologetically, "that's my decision."

"But—be living a *fantasy!*" Kroll squawked.

"I mean…sure. But with the memory-suppressant on, I won't *know* it's a fantasy."

"But—!"

"Look," Reg interrupted, "I get it, okay? The idea of me pissing away what little life I have left inside a computer-generated game obviously offends you on various levels. But there's nothing left for me out in the real world. I'm already dying of both old age and genetic disrepair, and any friends and family I had must be long gone by now. And there's nothing I can contribute that'll help preserve humanity, even assuming humanity could be saved at all. So…I think I'll just stay in the game. Once again, thanks for…looking in on us, I guess. But please, just let me re-engage with the game. Leave me here and go."

"But…*IS NOT REAL!!!*"

"It's real enough for me," Reg said softly. "And that's all that really matters."

"But—!"

"Game reset!" Reg commanded.

The cockpit vanished.

"…and deliver us from primal urges. Praise be to Qandho."

"Praise be to Qandho."

"General reports," Kroll said in his native tongue, glancing around the table at his subordinates. "Genetics?"

"Nothing new to report, Commander."

"Medical?"

"Aside from our impending extinction? Absolutely fantastic."

Kroll narrowed every single one of his eyes. "Let's keep things professional, shall we?"

"Apologies, Commander."

"Better. Engineering?"

"All good, Commander."

"Security?"

The chief security officer hesitated a moment. "Unfortunately, Commander, there's growing unrest amongst the crew of all fleet vessels. Cases of assault and public brawling are on the rise." He glanced sideways at the head of the genetics division. "Evidence suggests this is largely due to frustration over the recently announced failure of the latest round of fertility treatments, with over-promising of results by the Genetics Division leading to—"

The geneticist lunged at the security officer, hissing furiously, pincers raised.

"Control yourself!" Kroll snapped.

The geneticist bristled momentarily, then grudgingly bowed his head. "Apologies, Commander."

"Isn't it bad enough that our entire species is dying slowly from genetic collapse," Kroll growled, "without attempting to speed our extinction by indulging our primal urges? *Shrakha!* You should be leading by example, not acting like a bunch of stupid, squabbling hatchlings!" He glared around the table. His subordinates glared back, fighting the urge to physically defend their honour. Kroll nodded, satisfied that protocol had triumphed over instinct. "Going forward, the genetics division needs to run any updates through me before making public announcements. Okay? Right. Now, does anyone have anything further to add? No? In that case, I need suggestions on this wretched human, Reg Prescott. You've all read the briefing about him insisting upon remaining in the game to die rather than face reality, which is completely nuts. So—any ideas?"

"Couldn't we just forcibly disconnect him?" the security officer asked.

Kroll regarded the head of the medical division. "Well?"

The doctor shook his head. "Available information suggests there's danger of major psychological damage if we just yank him out of there. Even the relatively gentle intrusion we previously actioned almost gave him a conniption fit, so forcing him out..." He shrugged. "It seems to be a feature of the game itself, though perhaps not an intended one. The tech's relatively primitive and invasive, so physically disconnecting the player without going through certain protocols could even cause physiological damage. Under normal circumstances the game would judge when the player needed to exit the system—pre-set timing, external emergencies, the need for nutrition, etcetera—but the Earthly A.I.s rewired things so that the player never gets woken up, so to speak, as the A.I.s never intended humanity to ever exit the system again."

Kroll looked to the head of engineering. "Could we override that element of the system?"

"Probably. But as the doctor already mentioned, we're not just dealing with a mechanism here. I couldn't vouch for us being able to avoid damage to the players, even if the disconnection safeguards are deactivated."

The security officer raised a pincer. "The game he's in has multiplayer capacity, doesn't it? But he's playing solo, so doesn't that indicate an abnormal mentality for a human? Maybe the other players are more social, so could we look at contacting other humans instead."

Kroll and the doctor shared a look.

"What?" the security officer asked.

The doctor sighed. "We've taken a cursory look at the other players, and every single one of them is playing solo, so while the games were clearly made to accommodate social behaviours..." He shrugged. "Maybe the genetic crisis triggered a widespread psychological change? Anyway, from what we've observed of other players, Reg Prescott is likely to be as amenable to leaving the game as any other human, so it's probably a better allocation of time and resources to keep working on him than to start from the beginning with other players."

"Isn't there a human scientist we could talk to, at least?" the geneticist asked. "Someone who could better assist with *our* crisis?"

The doctor sighed. "Unfortunately, there's literally nobody any better qualified to assist among the remaining humans than Reg Prescott."

"Oh. Really? And what are *his* qualifications?"

"Something called a Bachelor of Arts in Theatre Studies, and ten years working as an Uber driver."

"What does all that mean?" the geneticist asked.

Kroll explained, and a gloomy silence fell across the table.

"Perhaps..." The doctor hesitated. "Our previous intrusion upon Reg Prescott's gameplay, while upsetting to him, didn't seem to cause any *major* psychological damage, possibly because it was actioned within the game only. We didn't attempt to physically extricate him. Maybe if we keep explaining how foolish he's being by denying reality and wasting his life—"

"He didn't exactly respond well last time."

"Yes, but if we kept at him, and also permanently disconnected the memory-suppressant, he might get so sick of the game that he'd leave of his own volition. And then we could roll the same process out to the rest of the humans."

"Do you think that would work?"

The doctor shrugged again. "I mean, Reg Prescott seems like a thoroughly stubborn bastard, and it's fair to assume it may be a trait common to all members of his species. So it might work, or it might not. But I'd suggest we give it the briefest of trials, and if it doesn't work we drop the whole thing as a bad job, and…you know…"

Kroll eyed the doctor sternly. "And what?"

"Well, you know. Leave."

"And why exactly are you so keen to move on from Earth? The flares won't enter their final phase for almost another year."

The doctor glanced around at his colleagues, who all suddenly developed a deep fascination with the table-top. He coughed nervously. "Commander, if I may speak freely?"

"I wish you would."

"Well, it's just that—and I hope my colleagues here will back me up on this—I think most aboard the fleet would admit that it's always difficult to suppress our primal urges, but that the mission to Earth—bringing with it hope for a possible solution to our issues—provided an alternate focus. A much-needed distraction. In addition to Qandho, of course," he added hurriedly, noting Kroll's expression. "But…we know that mission's over now. And we'll have to announce that to the fleet sooner or later. And once we do…well, we've already heard from my colleague here about what loss of hope does to fleet morale." The doctor nodded towards the security officer. "So the sooner we can retrieve these humans from the game, the sooner we can move on, and the sooner you can formulate and announce a new mission to focus upon. And if we *can't* get the humans to leave the game, I think we should probably—"

Kroll leaned forwards, smiling pleasantly. "Who's the Commander here?"

The doctor bowed his head, pouting. "You, Commander."

"Correct. I'm also, you'll no doubt recall, the appointed Most Holy Mouthpiece of Qandho for this fleet, and the Gospel of Qandho dictates our sacred duty is to preserve life, which the retrieval of these humans from their gaming system achieves."

"I—"

"And obviously," Kroll continued, "that means to suggest any course of action in opposition to those sacred duties would count as—" he glanced around the table, "—anyone? Anyone?—*BLASPHEMY!*" he roared, slamming his pincers down against the table and glaring at the doctor.

Silence.

"So," Kroll continued amiably, "in a nutshell, we leave Earth when *I* say. Understood?"

The doctor glared resentfully back at his commander.

Kroll felt a pang of regret. He and the doctor had been good friends once. But the responsibilities of leadership outweighed the niceties and comforts of personal relationships. "So—we'll follow the path you first suggested: disengage the memory-suppressant, and provide ongoing counselling to Reg Prescott on the necessity of vacating the game. Okay?"

"Yes, Commander." The doctor paused. "I…do have an additional suggestion."

"Yes?"

"We provide the counselling via direct visual communication rather than just the in-game audio previously accessed."

"Visual?" the engineer queried. "You mean, enter the game ourselves?"

The doctor nodded. "Exactly. Thus providing a virtual persona for the humans to relate to."

Kroll glanced at the engineer.

"Can we do that? Adjust the necessary connections to Arthrod physiology?"

"I don't see why not."

Kroll glanced back at the doctor. "And you really feel there's an advantage to doing this?"

"Absolutely. It'll make the counselling more impactful by being more personal. More acceptable. More relaxing."

Hiding behind the lavatory door, Lars was just about to leap out and bushwhack the trooper who was answering the call of nature when something utterly nightmarish materialised in front of him.

"*AAAAAAAAAAAAAAAARGH!*" Lars screamed, then paused, looking the monstrosity up and down. "*AAAAAAAAAAAAAAAARGH!*" he reiterated.

Three metres tall and mantled in a spiny black exoskeleton, the creature stood upon two powerful legs, while four massive arms terminating in crab-like pincers extended from the shoulders. The head was vaguely bug-like, an unsettling number of oversized boiled-fish eyes peering at Lars—Reg—from above a gaping, fang-filled mouth.

"Not think you react so badly," it said mildly.

Reg swallowed heavily. "Kroll?" He cleared his throat. "You, er...took me by surprise, that's all. What are you doing here? I thought we'd said our goodbyes—oh, crap!"

The trooper, momentarily stunned by the unexpected violation of his privacy, had finally recovered his wits sufficiently to draw his sidearm and start shooting. Kroll bellowed as a barrage of laser-fire tore into his body.

"Reset scene!" Reg snapped, pushing his way out from behind the door. The room flickered. The trooper vanished.

Kroll glanced down as his wounds healed. "Can do anytime during game?"

"Only if you happen to *remember* you're playing a game! Look at that!" Reg said sourly, gesturing around the room. "Look at the crappy definition! It's like watching Community TV! And this!" He held up his aged hands. "I look like I've been in the bloody bath too long! I already know I'm old, I don't need reminding of that, but the game's been ignoring my commands to revert back to my gaming avatar! How come?"

"Safety feature. You in game long time, and still have self-image of you as young man, so if you left game still believing you young you suffer shock when see true self. Normally is short period after game when reality bleed through to game as memory-suppressant shut down, in preparation of leaving, to give time to deal with reality."

Reg scowled. "Yeah, well, I'm *not* leaving, am I? So why aren't the gaming avatar and memory-suppressant still operating?"

"Because we switch off."

Reg gritted his teeth. "And why the hell would you do that?"

"Because," Kroll growled, *"none of this real! You need to leave!"*

"Christ! Why does that bug you so much?" Reg snapped. "I *know* it's just a game, but I *don't care!* It's none of your bloody concern anyway, so will you please just re-install the memory-suppressant and go away?"

"Against dictates of Qandho! You stay, you die!"

"I'm going to die anyway, you idiot!"

"But if return to reality, you get to live real life! Qandho dictate we preserve life, no matter how short! To waste remaining life in game is *blasphemous!"*

"GET OUT!" Reg screamed, taking a swing at Kroll. *"GET OUT, YOU SELF-RIGHTEOUS PRICK!"*

Kroll jumped back, instinctively assuming a defensive stance. "I go!" he snarled, fighting down the urge to attack. "But be back! Player Two, disengage!"

The doctor and engineer studiously avoided making eye contact with Kroll as the Commander sat up on the couch, yanking the gamelink from his skull. *"Shrakha!* This damned human needs a kick to the cranium!"

The doctor shrugged. "I mean, we're dealing with an alien psychology, Commander. Perhaps we need to consider taking a different approach, regardless of the commands of Qandho..." He paused, regarding the game display as Lars Janssen dispatched a squad of Nazi troopers with an agency-issue pen-knife.

Kroll coughed pointedly.

The doctor started. "Apologies, Commander. I was, er…the game is really quite interesting. From a psychological point-of-view, I mean."

Kroll eyed the doctor suspiciously. Increasingly, there were times when his subordinates' focus seemed to be slipping, and Kroll already had too much on his plate to worry about such things. Just that morning there had been two deaths amongst the crew due to 'natural causes,' an increasingly-used euphemism for genetic collapse. "Do you have any suggestions? Either of you?"

The engineer shook his head. "I'm just here to facilitate the hook up of the system to Arthrod physiology, Commander."

"Then consider yourself dismissed. And what about you?" Kroll asked the doctor, as the engineer left.

"Well, Commander, I know I suggested having us enter the game to make the counselling process more effective…but what if, instead of reasoning with him, we actually made an effort to *increase* his frustration over the disconnection of the memory-suppressant, thereby pressuring him to quit the game of his own volition?"

An evil grin slowly spread across Kroll's face.

"By ze time we have finished with you," the torturer gloated, "you vill *beg* to die! But first, you vill tell us *everything!*"

Tied to a chair, Lars squirmed in apparent discomfort as he surreptitiously slid the tiny thermal lance from under the callus on his palm. "Had an extra bowl of Sadistic Bastard Flakes this morning, did we?" he croaked, furtively cutting through his bonds. "Well, you'll get nothing from me, Nazi scum!"

The torturer leaned over him, grinning. "Vant to bet?" he hissed, and was extremely surprised when, a moment later, Lars jammed the lance up against his throat, cutting it from ear to ear.

The sentry by the door snapped into action as the torturer fell, swinging his rifle around to cover Lars. Lars froze, knowing he had no chance to move before the sentry pulled the trigger—

K-chunk!

Lars smiled pleasantly. "Hi. Rifle jammed?"

"Oh, *scheisse*," the trooper muttered resignedly.

Biff! Crack! Snap!

Lars dusted his hands off. "Sorry to beat and run, but—"

"*BOO!*" a voice yelled in his ear.

Reg shrieked.

Kroll grinned maliciously. "How you even derive pleasure from game? No challenge! Guard's rifle jam at crucial moment? Use knife to kill entire squad armed with guns?"

"They were…really bad shots! Look," Reg snapped, "I'm not leaving, so bugger off! You're interrupting my game!"

"No fun when reminded not real? Hardly worth staying…"

Reg folded his arms across his chest and glared at Kroll. "We both know you can't just shut down the game, which is why you're trying to force me out with this…douchebaggery. But listen, Kroll—I have absolutely no intention of leaving. In fact, I positively look forward to dying in here!"

Kroll's smirk vanished. "*SHRAKHA!*" he screamed, practically foaming at the mouth. "Make mockery of Qandho! I drag you out, no matter how long it take or what others say!"

"What others?" Reg narrowed his eyes. There was a long, awkward pause. "So…someone else is having an issue with your insistence that I leave the game? Who? Your crew? Your officers?"

"Is…*hypothetical* others!" Kroll snapped

"Oh. I *see*." Reg smiled smugly. "So the Commander's having problems with his staff, eh? I shouldn't be surprised, really. Patience obviously isn't a virtue amongst your people, if *your* temper's anything to go by. That makes sense: you're a former warrior race with aggressive instincts probably hardwired, and demonstrably short fuses…" His eyes narrowed again. "Qandho isn't the real problem, is it? I'm going to die whatever I do, and I don't think you're such a religious zealot that you really believe it makes a difference whether I die in here or out there. No, I think what's really got you stressed is that your crew are beginning to get aggressive about the effort you're putting into retrieving me."

Kroll's pincers began to burn. "Not stand here, listen to such *shrakha!*" he snapped. "Player Two, disengage!"

Alone again, Reg leaned back against the wall, pressing his fingers against the cool, smooth tiles. *Not real.*

Am I wrong to want to stay here? To piss away my remaining existence in a computer-generated fantasy when I could be out there doing something that impacts upon the real world? Something worthwhile, perhaps? Maybe even contributing to solving our sterility issues somehow?

No. That's a pipe dream. Even the A.I.s couldn't help us.

Nonetheless, a real life. And wouldn't a real life be its own reward?

He glanced around the computer-generated bathroom.

But with the memory-suppressant on, this *could all be as good as real. I could make a real difference* here. *As far as I'd ever know…*

Reg smiled sadly.

"What the frek is going on here?" Kroll snapped, pulling out his gamelink.

"Commander?" The doctor's expression was one of hatchling-like innocence, as the two functionaries standing at his shoulder tried to sidle away unnoticed.

"Don't play dumb with me! This is a restricted area!" Kroll glared at the functionaries. "If I see either of you in here again without permission, I'll have your carapaces steamed! Get out!"

The functionaries scuttled away, bowing and scraping apologetically.

The doctor assumed a defensive stance. "Apologies, Commander. They, er, asked to see the game, and—"

"*Shrakha!* We restricted access to everything pertaining to the humans and their gameplay *specifically* to prevent exposure of the crew to aggressive displays! Do you think I make decisions like this just to amuse myself? I'm trying to stop the crew from killing one another, you idiot!" Kroll's communicator bleeped. "Yes?"

"Security. I'm sorry to report there's been another incident, Commander, with three deaths resulting."

Kroll sighed inwardly, feeling ill. "Another brawl?"

"Yes, Commander."

"Understood. Have a full report to me as soon as possible. Kroll out." Kroll eyed the doctor murderously. "*This* is why we restrict access!"

The doctor shuffled nervously. "Permission to speak frankly, Commander?"

"Go on."

"Look, the crew isn't stupid, Commander. They—*we*—fully recognise the danger of indulging our primal urges, and we're all mostly capable of modifying our behaviour accordingly." The doctor hesitated. "But…"

"What? Get to the point!"

"Well…everyone's already hugely stressed, what with the ongoing health crisis, and the news that the humans don't have any solutions for us. And with the added stress caused by your rigid discipline, and the perception by some that this focus upon dragging the remaining humans out of their gaming systems is a waste of time that's only delaying us from leaving Earth, well…maybe, I don't know…maybe it'd be an idea to…ease off?"

Kroll felt a cold rage bubbling up inside him. His claws burned. "Get. Out," he hissed quietly, desperately fighting the urge to tear the doctor apart.

Growling nervously, the doctor backed out of the room.

I can barely control my own urges! Kroll chastised himself. *How can I expect better from my people?* The faces of long-dead friends and family flitted before his mind's eye. Genetic diseases. Violence. *Not me! Not my people! We* will *overcome these trials, save our species, rescue the humans! Qandho will shine a light upon the way!*

We cannot give up hope…

Trembling with fear and shame and anger, Kroll turned, his attention wandering to the game display. Lars Janssen was desperately attempting to steer a burning Nazi cargo ship from what seemed to be inevitable impact with a rapidly approaching wharf, panicking figures fleeing the dock as the vessel careened forwards through churning waves. Three seconds to impact! Two! One!

"Commander?"

Kroll started as the security officer strode into the room. "Yes?" he snapped.

"I've submitted my report to your comms, Commander. I thought perhaps we could discuss it in person. At your convenience, of course," the officer added, glancing pointedly at the game display.

"I've…not had a chance to look at it yet, but we can discuss the essentials right now." Kroll took a moment to collect himself. "So. What are you doing to prevent further violence amongst the crew? Specifically, I mean?"

The security officer hesitated. "Well…obviously that's one of the things I wanted to discuss with you, Commander. Current measures aren't proving as effective as they once were, so—"

"So impose new measures!"

"Commander?"

"It's a simple enough directive, isn't it? Use your initiative!"

The security officer hesitated again. "With respect, Commander, your recent leadership hasn't allowed much room for…*initiative*. You've been tightening your control over pretty much all aspects of fleet operation, instead of allowing your staff to do their jobs. And we *do* know how to do our jobs, Commander."

"Insolence!" Kroll hissed.

"I'm merely stating facts, Commander." The officer shifted subtly in a way that, Kroll realised, would better allow him to defend himself should his commander decide to attack.

"So. You've decided to use my directives as an excuse to, what? Do nothing?"

"Qandho forbid, Commander." The officer glanced again at the gaming display. "And again with respect, I think perhaps that's part of the problem."

Kroll seethed, inching forward as he prepared to—

What the frek am I doing??

Kroll abruptly turned his back on the security officer. "You're dismissed. I shall expect a more satisfactory plan of action from you at the next division heads meeting tomorrow. Now go!"

There was a long pause.

Kroll turned back to glare at the security officer. "Yes?" he asked coldly.

"I've been asked to pass on a message to you, Commander. From the bulk of the crew, and all of the division heads and officers."

Kroll braced himself. "Well?"

"It's a formal request for you to authorise departure of the fleet from Earth, Commander. Immediately."

"Indeed. Or what?"

The security officer's tone was neutral. "I can only speak for those already proposing action, Commander, either publicly or in discussion with myself. But I feel a decent summation is that failure to comply with the aforementioned request will further undermine the ability of your people to repress their instinctive aggression. That said, at your behest, everyone has been looking to the directives of Qandho as a means of sublimating our natural urges, but..." he shrugged, "speaking frankly—and yet again, with respect—it's not going to be enough to prevent what might happen next."

"You're speaking blasphemy!" Kroll whispered, now so angry that he was actually smiling. "Qandho dictates that we stay to retrieve the humans—so we do not leave until that goal is achieved. Now...*go and make that directive understood to all.* Do you understand?" His tone brooked no further opposition.

The two angry crustaceans eyeballed each other, an activity for which both were amply equipped. Eventually the security officer bowed his head. "Understood, Commander."

"Now get out of my sight!"

Kroll's claws continued to quiver long after the security officer had departed.

The creature standing on the far side of the combat pit was big, ugly, and had more sets of claws, teeth and spines than the entire menagerie of a masochists' petting zoo. Lars had never seen one before, but there was a vivid description of this particular beastie in the IAASNA Handbook under 'Things To Avoid': a Venusian Shanghorn.

"And me without a perigosto stick," Lars muttered. He tensed, ready to move. Shanghorns were fast, powerful, aggressive, and—worst of all—smart enough to recognise their position at the top of the food-chain, which meant they gave not a single crap about niceties such as caution or restraint when hunting down their prey, which included everything.

Without warning, the Shanghorn pounced. Lars took off around the perimeter of the pit with the beast in hot pursuit. His mind raced. According to the handbook, Shanghorns had only one weakness; a major nerve centre located between the eyes, a blow to which would induce instant paralysis. A perigosto stick would have been ideally suited to the task of hitting that nerve centre. But Lars didn't have a perigosto stick. He didn't even have a pea-shooter. He glanced around desperately. Was there *anything* in the pit he could use as a weapon?

Nothing but hot sand, burning under his feet—

Hot sand? Heat? Perspiration?

Lars glanced down at his sweat-soaked trousers, and an idea came to him. Grabbing his waistband with both hands as he ran, he gave a mighty tug, tearing his trousers off. Gripping one of the leg cuffs, Lars rotated his wrist in a lassoing gesture, twisting the sodden pants into a heavy, rope-like length. He glanced back. The Shanghorn was almost upon him. Giving the trouser-rope one last twist, Lars skidded to a halt and spun around to face his pursuer. As the beast flew at him, Lars drew his hand back then snapped it upwards, flicking the end of the rope directly between the Shanghorn's eyes.

Thwack!

There was a pause. Then, with a moan, the Shanghorn toppled over and crashed to the ground.

The universe flickered.

"*LEAVE GAME!*" Kroll roared. "Not ask again! Not let you die! Not fail in my duty!"

Reg rubbed his brow wearily. "Look, for the last time—*I am not leaving*, so *PISS OFF!*"

"Cannot do! Qandho not allow! Why you not understand??"

"Qandho, Qandho, Qandho!" Reg sneered. "Stop hiding behind your faith, Kroll! The only thing stopping you from leaving me here is *you!* You can't get the Earthling to bend to your will, but you're too proud to admit defeat! Too proud to let your subordinates see you fail, even though they don't actually care if you succeed! In the end, the only thing that matters to you is that you're in the right! And do you know what else? Deep down, I don't think you actually give a single crap about Qandho!"

Kroll gasped. "You take back!"

"You're just using your religion as a means to justify your actions! And that makes you a bad person!"

"*SILENCE!*"

Reg grinned savagely. "You heard me! You're a bad person, and you should feel bad!"

Kroll hissed furiously. "I tear you apart!"

"Go on, then!"

Kroll trembled, torn between instinct and religious directive. "Qandho not permit!"

"Yeah?" Reg raised his voice. "Acquire razor-tipped staff!" Without giving Kroll a chance to react, Reg lashed out with the weapon that had suddenly appeared in his hand.

104

Kroll screamed as a pincer-tip fell to the sand, jetting black goo. Hormones surged. Reason gave way to primal rage. Shrieking maniacally, he attacked.

Standing his ground, Reg thrust the tip of his weapon forward, driving the blade deep into Kroll's guts. Kroll bellowed and slammed a pincer down on the staff. Reg staggered back against the wall of the pit clutching a handful of kindling, while Kroll tore the blade from his bleeding stomach. Tossing it aside, he drove a pincer into the wall either side of Reg, caging him. Reg sprang up into the air, executed a perfect summersault, and landed squarely on Kroll's back. Kroll reared up, turning towards the centre of the pit, then bucked forwards. Before Reg could jump free, the buck became a roll, and Kroll tumbled head-first across the floor of the pit, crushing his human opponent into the sand with all the weight and destructive power of a charging rhino.

Crunch!

Kroll sprang to his feet, spun around, and began to slam his pincers down repeatedly upon the broken form lying on the ground, crushing bones to jelly and bursting organs, splattering gore across the sand. After almost a minute the blood-lust began to fade and Kroll stepped back, panting as his muscles relaxed. Slowly his mind began to clear…

What have I done?

There was a long, long silence.

Eventually, the universe flickered. The shattered corpse vanished, and Reg—whole again—appeared standing beside Kroll,

"Why you force me to do this?" Kroll asked dully. "Belief that we could suppress urges the only thing keep us going. If suppress instincts, perhaps can suppress genetic decay. But now…" He sighed. "When word spread of what I do, dictates of Qandho will be…worthless. Without faith, aggression increase." He shook his head hopelessly. "You doom us all. *I* doom us all."

"Felt good, though, didn't it?" Reg lowered himself into a seated position on the sand. "The thrill of combat, of naked aggression. Can't be healthy, fighting those primal urges. You're an angry species, Kroll. The instinct to fight is probably nature's way of allowing you to let off steam so you don't go completely psychotic."

Kroll bowed his head. "And now nature condemn us. Sterility inevitably kill us, but aggression speed extinction." He sat down disconsolately next to Reg. For a few minutes neither of them spoke, both simply gazing up at the huge, pale, computer-generated sun overhead.

Eventually, Reg shrugged regretfully. "*Everything* dies, Kroll. Every*thing* and every*one*. You. Me. Humanity. The Arthrod. We don't get a choice in that. But we can choose how we go out. We can choose to loosen up and enjoy whatever time we have left, or keep going through all the pointless little motions of trying to halt the inevitable."

"You give this some thought," Kroll noted.

"Yeah, well, it's hard to not spend time thinking about this whole situation when the memory-suppressant's been disconnected. Even with the distraction of the game." Reg gave Kroll an appraising look. "I do have a suggestion to make."

Kroll glanced at him. "Which is?"

Reg told him.

There was a very long silence.

"But…" Kroll said eventually, then trailed off.

"But what? Can you give me one genuinely good reason why not?"

They continued to sit staring up at the sun while Kroll tried to think of one genuinely good reason why not…

Kroll sat up on the couch, carefully pulling the gamelink from his head. For a moment he said nothing, staring contemplatively into the middle distance.

"Commander?" the doctor prompted eventually.

Kroll turned to look at him. "You were watching, of course?"

"Yes, Commander."

Kroll nodded, then glanced towards the door. "How many others?"

"I, er—"

Kroll waved a claw dismissively. "It's fine. I'm guessing that keeping them out must be like attempting to hold back a cosmic storm with an umbrella. But…I do think that perhaps I need to make an announcement sooner rather than later, given that word is almost certainly already spreading as we speak." He gave the doctor a long, hard look. "Don't you agree?"

The doctor considered his words carefully. "I believe that may be the best course of action, Commander."

Kroll sighed. "I'll schedule a meeting for all division heads and officers immediately, followed by a fleet-wide broadcast once we've agreed upon some basic actions going forward." He paused. "I wonder, though…"

"What, Commander?"

"Well, it's probably more of a question for the head of engineering, but…these human gaming systems…"

"Yes, Commander?"

"Well, I wonder how many players their multiplayer mode can accommodate at any given time?"

Lars sighed as he regarded his surroundings; the inside of the vast bunker, the legion of Nazi troopers aiming their rifles at his head, and the bizarre mechanical object standing in front of him. The thing was roughly the size and shape of a watermelon, with four spider-like legs projecting from the lower hemisphere. The upper half was a clear, fluid-filled dome in which floated a grisly lump of crenulated flesh.

"What's this?" Lars asked. "Bring Your Offal to Work Day?"

"Insolence!" A buzzing voice emanated from the mechanism. "I must remember to remove zat tongue of yours before you die!"

Lars raised an eyebrow. "I don't recognise the voice, but the overacting's familiar. *Hottschtepper? Is that you?*"

"*Yessss!*" the mechanism hissed. "You may have destroyed my body when you blew up my KillMoon, Janssen…but my brain now controls zis MindenValker!"

"Huh. Glad to see you didn't lose your looks."

"Laugh while you may, Janssen! Zis time, there is no escape!"

Lars shrugged. "If you say so." He paused. "Although…"

"Vhat?" Hottschtepper snapped suspiciously.

"Oh, just that there are two things I should mention before you choke on your own smugness. Firstly, you *really* should get the optics on your MindenValker checked, because you obviously haven't noticed that I'm holding a primed sunflare incendiary device." He slowly held the object aloft. "If I drop this, you can kiss your metal arse goodbye."

Muttering, the troopers drew back.

Hottschtepper fumed incoherently for a moment, then growled: "And ze second thing?"

Lars smiled, then let out a piercing whistle.

Immediately, hundreds of massive, crablike beings began to tear their way into the bunker, ripping effortlessly through reinforced walls, scuttling in every direction as they took up pre-planned positions around the perimeter, where they sat waiting, pincers quivering in anticipation.

The troopers covering Lars immediately lost interest in the agent, pointing their weapons in all directions, unsure of where to aim.

"Assume defensive positions!" Hottschtepper screamed.

The mob of panicking troopers parted as one of the creatures strode towards Lars, regarding the agent amusedly. "Need hand?"

Lars grinned. "Gentlemen, Hottschtepper—may I present Commodore Krotek of the Glorious Arachnoid Empire!"

"*Destroy zem!*" Hottschtepper screamed. "*Destroy zem all!*"

Lars sighed. "You talk too much." He touched a button on the base of the sunflare and the device morphed into something resembling a sonic disrupter, and for the best possible reason. "Part of our new TransMuter range," he explained, taking aim. "Enjoy!"

The disrupter burped softly. Hottschtepper let out a single outraged squawk. Then his brain imploded, spattering the inside of the MindenValker's dome. The mechanism staggered about like a drunken crab for moment, then fell over with a crash and lay still, as dead as its occupant.

A collective moan went up from the assembled Nazi forces.

"Hey!" Lars yelled.

A thousand rifles swung around to cover him. The Arachnoids tensed.

"I've got just one thing to say," Lars continued, then paused for effect before shouting: "*LET'S KICK SOME NAZI ASS!*"

With a roar the Arachnoids swept forward, cutting into the Nazi troopers like Shanghorns into, well, pretty much anything that got in their way. Rifles blazed. Pincers rose and fell. Blood, limbs and internal organs flew in all directions as the troopers screamed and died.

Lars and Krotek stood surveying the chaos for a moment. Then a rifle blast parted the air between them.

"An agent's job is never done!" Lars shouted above the din.

Krotek gestured invitingly. "After you?"

Lars opened his mouth to reply…then hesitated as something tickled the back of his mind; a vague sense of something forgotten. There was a flicker of images. A flaring sun. An old man lying on a bed. He frowned, grasping, trying to remember, but it was like moving through a dark and unfamiliar house, opening one dilapidated door after another, endlessly searching, until—

And then, abruptly, it was gone.

Lars blinked, shaking his head. "Sorry—what?"

"I say," Kroll growled, "is time to join party?"

Lars grinned. "Sure. Why not?" Gripping his disrupter tightly, he took a deep breath. "*ALIEN SPACE NAZIS MUST DIE!*" he yelled joyously, and he and Krotek leapt once more into the fray.

Conquest

The vast alien spacecraft plunged downwards through the atmosphere and came to a screeching halt (figuratively speaking) just above Parliament House in Canberra, hovering silently in the air like an enormous floating thing. Moments later every TV set, PC, laptop, tablet and smartphone worldwide turned itself on, revealing the image of a hideous, octopoid alien equipped with far too many eyes and teeth.

"Earthlings!" the creature snarled. "In order to avoid a practical demonstration of superior Zrrgon firepower, we strongly urge you to comply with our one, simple demand!

"*We want your women!*"

The response from local military forces was immediate and merciless.

When the smoke cleared, Canberra was gone. The spaceship, however, very much wasn't.

"Imbeciles!" the Zrrgon spokesthing snarled. "Try that again, and we'll vaporise something important! Now—we want your women! Immediately! Twenty thousand of them, whether biologically so or identifying as such, and representing every race, creed and colour upon this miserable planet, to be assembled beneath our ship exactly one

Earthly week from today! Failure to comply—well, you get the idea. Oh, and we demand the loan of a lectern as well! Thanks!" Cackling maniacally, the spokesthing terminated communications, and the kids were finally able to access TikTok again.

The public response worldwide was of absolute outrage. The aliens want our *women??* For what terrible purpose?? As sex-slaves?? As incubators for hideous alien larvae?? The possibilities raised were all pretty horrifying, and citizens everywhere desperately lobbied their governments to reject the Zrrgons' demand.

Unfortunately, the governments of Earth didn't feel they had much choice in the matter. Not if they wanted to be around for the next round of elections, anyway.

And so, a week later, twenty thousand women stood in the shallow crater beneath the hovering Zrrgon spacecraft, all nervously awaiting their fate.

With a deep rumble worthy of the Industrial Light & Magic audio workshop, the bottom of the spacecraft irised open and the Zrrgon spokesthing came floating down to earth in a beam of light. Drooling with lustful anticipation, the spokesthing squelched over to the lectern—thoughtfully provided by the (former) supplier of office furniture to the (former) Australian government—and moistly cleared its multitude of throats.

"Greetings!" it gargled. "Now, I suppose you wretched Earthwomen are wondering exactly what the Zrrgon have in store for you! Well—wonder no more!"

An orifice in the spokesthing's side opened, disgorging a slime-coated, metal attaché case.

"*The Zrrgon are here to conquer Earth!*" the spokesthing gloated. "And you, Earthwomen, will be the *instruments* of that conquest!"

With a sinister *Click!,* the case opened.

The crowd drew back with a collective moan.

The spokesthing reached into the case and pulled out a small glass vial, which it held aloft for all to see.

"Behold!" it drooled. "The Dermatone XK5—scientifically proven to reverse dermal aging in over two thousand known sentient species!"

Slowly, as though hypnotised, the crowd edged forwards, all eyes fixed upon the vial.

"The recommended retail price in your local currency is seventy-nine dollars and ninety-nine cents," the spokesthing continued in a very businesslike tone, "but if you ladies sign up as distributors for Zrrgonetics today, the price for you is only twenty-eight dollars and forty-three cents per unit, plus you'll receive—at absolutely no additional cost—this handy and attractive branded carry case..."

Tools of the Trade

Clart blinked the sweat from his eyes, and ran a trembling finger down the directory screen until he found what he was looking for:

Pestex Universal™
Natural Pest Control

Clart tapped the ad, then pulled an antibacterial wipe from the dispenser on the wall, obsessively rubbing it over his hands as he waited. Eventually the image of a clean-cut young man dressed in a crisp, brown uniform appeared on the screen. The man gave Clart a pleasant smile.

"Thank you for calling Pestex Universal. This is Hale. How may I help you?"

Clart licked his dry lips. "Please!" he croaked. "It's an emergency! I've got *organisms* in my *home!*"

Hale nodded gravely. "I see. Home infestation. Could you describe the issue in a little more detail? Have you actually *seen* the invasive organisms?"

"It was just the odd bit of detritus on the floor at first, so I assumed the home cleaning system required a service, but after the service the detritus kept appearing, and then…and then, today, I saw something scuttle across the floor!" Clart grabbed another wipe and dabbed his forehead with it, feeling ill.

"I see. Well, the first thing to remember is not to panic, Mister…" Hale consulted the screen at his end, "…Clart? I assume you wish us to attend immediately, so may I have your condenser code, please? Thank you. I see you're just half a light-year away from us, so we'll be with you momentarily, Mister Clart."

A few minutes later the condenser in the corner of Clart's habitat pinged. Clart glanced at the entry request as it popped up and hit the Accept icon. The condenser flashed briefly, and a figure stepped from the tube, a black zippered compendium tucked under his arm. It was Hale.

"Nice to meet you in person, Mister Clart." Hale thrust out a gloved hand. Clart drew back, a horrified expression on his face. Hale nodded then unzipped and opened his compendium to reveal a tablet inside. "My apologies, Mister Clart. I just had to ascertain your level of biophobia. *Extreme…*" he murmured to himself, entering something into the tablet.

"I was expecting an android!" Clart babbled, retreating to the far corner of the room. "Don't you have automatons to do this sort of work?"

Hale smiled wryly. "I'm sorry, Mister Clart—we find that automatons aren't yet suited to this line of work. Too many variables and potential hazards. Maybe once humanity feels sufficiently secure in developing a genuine artificial intelligence, but for the moment—"

"It's ridiculous," Clart muttered. "In this day and age! At the very least, I'd have expected you to send a properly sterilised simulant. Never in a million years would I have expected another *person* to turn up, let alone someone who was performing the role of call operator just a few minutes ago, probably surrounded by other service employees, all jammed into a single, cramped, unhygienic workspace! Surely there are laws against this sort of thing?"

Hale nodded. "I quite understand your feelings on the matter, Mister Clart. But it's all completely legal. And, for what it's worth, I underwent full decontamination before arriving. And as far as me working the company call centre—well, I'm actually the sole employee of your local Pestex Universal franchise. Owner, manager, receptionist, and general all-rounder. I do apologise if I gave the impression that this was more than just a one-man band, so to speak. But we do attempt to balance the shortage of company representatives with genuine old-fashioned service, delivered with a smile, and with everything done according to our manual. Which reminds me—" he took a moment to clear his throat, "—may I just take this opportunity to say how grateful we are that you've chosen Pestex Universal to—"

"It's not as though I had much choice in the matter!" Clart snapped. "You're the only pest control company listed for the entire local cluster!"

Hale nodded sadly. "It's a social thing, I'm afraid. Biophobia is the social norm across most of Human Space nowadays. Makes it terribly hard to recruit people into the pest control industry. The very thought of working around organisms gives most people the absolute horrors. It wouldn't matter so much if modern sterilisation techniques were more effective, but life can be surprisingly resistant. Sometimes it can infest or re-infest even the most sterile environments."

Clart stared at Hale. "So…even if you completely remove the organisms from my home, there's a chance they might…come back??"

Hale smiled regretfully.

Clart turned and gazed out of the lounge window at the featureless, concrete-smothered landscape beyond. This had once been a living moon, long deforested and poisoned, the atmosphere completely removed; rendered safe and sterile, just as it should be. But if he'd known there was even the tiniest chance of re-infestation, he'd never have left Orbital—

Hale coughed politely.

Clart blinked. "What?"

"Your contract?" Hale turned the open compendium around to face Clart, holding it out to display the tablet screen. "There's a full list of charges and terms of service in there, so if you could read it carefully and sign, we can begin."

Clart pulled a fresh wipe from a nearby dispenser. "Legal mumbo-jumbo," he muttered. "Why do I need to read this, anyway? It's a simple job, yes? You come in, kill the organisms, and leave. I don't care *how* you get the job done—I just want it *done!*" He quickly scrolled to the end of the contract and pressed his thumb against the relevant spot, then hurriedly handed the compendium back to Hale and wiped his hand clean. "There! Now can we *please* get on with it?"

Hale took a moment to cosign the contract, then closed the compendium and tucked it back under his arm. "Yes, of course. I've forwarded a copy of the contract to you for your reference. Now, let's find out what's bugging you, shall we? I'm terribly sorry," he added, without waiting for a reaction. "An old pest control joke. Would you like to show me the infestation site?"

Clart's expression was answer enough.

Hale nodded understandingly. "Well then, if you could give me an idea of where to look?"

Clart swallowed heavily. "Kitchen. Under the refrigeration unit"

"Right." Hale turned and walked quietly into the kitchen. After what seemed like ages he returned, nodding gravely. "Yes. Well, you were right to call us, Mister Clart. *Major* infestation in there. I wouldn't be surprised if they've gotten into the floors as well."

Clart felt nauseous. "Wh-what are they?"

"Cockroaches."

"*Cockroaches?!*" The unfamiliar word stuck in Clart's throat like a lump of bile.

"A household pest from Old Earth, believe it or not. Filthy, disease-carrying vermin. And very tough. They can live anywhere a human being can, and quite a few places we can't. If they get aboard a starship they can end up anywhere, and once the breeding cycle starts—oh, goodness!" Hale stepped forward and caught Clart as he fell, fainting. "Are you alright, Mister Clart?"

Clart's eyelids fluttered. "Wuh?" His hands flapped weakly, trying to push Hale away.

Hale eased Clart into a convenient chair. "It's okay, Mister Clart. If it makes you feel better, I don't think we'll have any trouble clearing out this infestation."

"Thank heavens!" Clart mumbled, grabbing a wipe and dabbing at the spots where Hale had touched him.

"I'll just pop back to the office and grab some tools, then I'll return and get the ball rolling. A few assassin bugs should solve the issue very effectively."

"Yes, please hurry, I—" Clart sat bolt upright in his chair. "Assassin bugs?"

"A species of Earthly insect that eats other insects. We release a small colony under your refrigerator, and—"

"*What?!*" Clart shrieked, jumping to his feet. "You want to bring *more* organisms into my home?!"

"They're genetically modified," Hale explained, "completely sterile, and programmed to die within five to six days of destroying the cockroaches."

"Absolutely not! Are you *insane?*"

Hale frowned. "And what do you propose we use instead, Mister Clart?"

"Well, chemicals of course! Poisons! The usual sort of thing!"

Hale shook his head. "Pestex Universal is a *natural* pest control company, Mister Clart. We don't use chemicals, only the occasional plant-based spray, and mostly other organisms that prey upon the invasive pests."

"Ridiculous!" spluttered Clart. "The companies that cleared this moon—"

"Didn't have to worry about preserving even the smallest part of the existing biosphere," Hale interjected. "They would have just completely razed it from orbit. Which was fine for wholesale sterilisation, but you can't employ techniques like that in an enclosed environment like this habitat, Mister Clart. Not without killing the human occupant as well."

"What??"

"It's all in the contract. You really should have read it properly."

"Oh, for—how can you possibly run a pest control company without using *pesticides?!*"

Hale shrugged apologetically. "Unfortunately there's nothing we can do about it. Pestex Universal has been around far longer that the current social norm of biophobia, and controlling pests through natural methods is one of the sacred cows of the company. Almost literally, as it happens. One of the founders was a Buddhist."

"Well, you're certainly not bringing any more organisms into *this* habitat!" Clart snapped.

Hale gave Clart a long, sad look. "Well," he said eventually, "I'm sorry, Mister Clart, but I don't think Pestex Universal will be able to help you after all." He turned and began to move towards the condenser.

"But…wait a minute!" said Clart desperately. "You can't just leave! *Please!* You've got to do *something!*"

"I'm sorry, Mister Clart, but if you won't let us use natural pest control methods…" Hale shrugged. "And I really don't think you'd be interested in the PM treatment, so—"

"Wait! Hang on! What's the PM treatment?"

"Well," Hale said hesitantly, "there's a service option for the client to receive light psychological modification to enable them to cope with the natural pest control methods we use. But if I may speak plainly, Mister Clart, your extreme level of biophobia leaves me doubting that you could bring yourself to undertake the process, knowing that doing so would make you amenable to the introduction of more organisms into your home."

Clart could feel another fainting fit coming on, and quickly lowered himself back into his chair. "This is a nightmare! Is there no way around this?"

Hale shrugged. "It really boils down to two very simple options. You can either undergo psychological modification and thereby reduce your biophobia to a point where you'll allow us to service you, or you can try to find a different pest control company in another cluster that'll agree to use less ecofriendly treatments in your home—which I imagine could take quite a while, assuming you could even find anyone at all—

and put up with what I can assure you will be a rapidly-increasing home infestation in the meantime." He paused. "I can't make this decision for you, Mister Clart. It's completely up to you."

There was a long silence. Clart withdrew another wipe from a dispenser and rubbed it over his shaking hands, considering his options.

"Mister Clart?"

"All right!" Clart snapped. "*Do* it! Give me the PM! And get those organisms out of my home!"

Hale nodded, retrieved the tablet from his bag, tapped a key, and held the tablet out to Clart. "Standard psychological modification terms and conditions. Read and sign, please…"

To Clart's slight relief the psychological modification proved to be completely painless, merely requiring him to sit for ten minutes while Hale used a slim, pen-like object to project pulses of light directly into Clart's eyes.

"Of course," Hale had cautioned, "this won't rid you of your phobia completely, merely tone it down to a tolerable level. It's never a good idea to mess with the mind any more than strictly necessary."

Following this, Hale jumped back to his office and soon returned carrying a small plastic box with numerous holes in the top. A skittering noise emanated from within. Clart backed away, regarding the box suspiciously.

"Try not to think of them as *organisms*," Hale advised, as he moved towards the kitchen. "Instead, consider them merely…*tools of the trade*."

Clart followed cautiously, watching from a safe distance as Hale got down on his knees, carefully opened the box, and tipped the contents out onto the kitchen floor. The sight of a dozen predatory insects scuttling away beneath the refrigerator immediately brought Clart out in a sweat, but at least he hadn't fainted, which seemed to indicate the psychological modification had been reasonably effective.

Hale waited until the last assassin bug vanished from sight, then clambered to his feet. "There we go," he said, moving past Clart into the living room. "That should take care of the infestation. Give the bugs a couple of days to eliminate the cockroaches, then another few days to die out themselves. Your cleaning system will take care of the remains, and the PM should allow you to use the refrigerator in the meantime without too much distress."

"Thank heavens!" Clart sighed.

"Well," Hale smiled, awkwardly nestling the empty box under his arm alongside the compendium, "may I say, on behalf of Pestex Universal, that it's a pleasure to have been of service to you. And now, if you'll excuse me—" He nodded politely, then moved towards the condenser.

"Wait a moment," Clart said. "Aren't you going to bill me for this?"

Hale turned, smiling broadly. "Not until the job's been fully completed, Mister Clart. It's all specified in the contract. Good old-fashioned service. We'll give you a courtesy call in around two weeks' time just to confirm the infestation's gone, then invoice you for services rendered. Hopefully you won't require our assistance again, but I do hope you'll recommend us to your friends." He nodded again. "Have a nice day, Mister Clart."

"You incompetent fool!" Clart gibbered, glaring at the image of Hale on the screen. "You promised...you said...!" He broke off, choking with rage.

Hale frowned. "I'm terribly sorry, Mister Clart—is there still a problem with the cockroaches?"

"A problem?? *Yes*, there's a problem, damn it! But not with the cockroaches! The cockroaches are all gone—but those assassin bugs are still running around all over the kitchen two weeks later! You said they'd be dead by now! *And* they've started breeding! There are little ones climbing the walls as we speak!"

"Well *that* shouldn't be possible!" Hale frowned. "Even if my supplier had mistakenly given me fertile stock, immature assassin bugs take at least two standard solar months to hatch from their eggs. Look, give me five minutes and I'll be right over to take a look."

"Yes," Hale said, nodding slowly, "I see. Well, this is certainly an issue."

"Which I expect you to fix right away!" Clart growled from the kitchen doorway, rubbing a wipe across his brow.

"Yes, well," Hale said, "I can completely understand your annoyance, Mister Clart. I'm annoyed also. As mentioned, our suppliers programmed those assassin bugs for complete sterility and a week-long lifespan."

"Well, obviously your suppliers messed up!"

"Hmm." Hale glanced around the kitchen, frowning. "Tell me, Mister Clart—what sort of sealant was used in the construction of your habitat?"

"What?" Clart stared incredulously at Hale. "How would I know? *Sealant* sealant! What the hell does that have to do with anything??"

Hale strode over to the kitchen window and peered intently at the frame. Then he opened his compendium and withdrew a small scanning device, which he waved over the frame for a moment before consulting the readout. "Ah."

"What?"

"Trisilicate HX—one of the sealants they used to use in construction on fully sterilised worlds, primarily to guard against re-infestation by moulds. It contains a mutagenic compound that destroys moulds by disrupting their genetic codes. However, they stopped using it after it turned out that some species of insect reacted very differently to the mutagen, often experiencing hyperfertility, even in stock programmed to be infertile, which is exactly what I'd suggest has happened with the assassin bugs here."

"That's all very well, but what are you going to do to fix the problem? This is still your responsibility!"

Hale rubbed the back of his neck. "Actually, Mister Clart, if you'd read your contract, you'd have noted a clause pertaining to the onus upon the client to disclose the presence of any materials within the home that might affect the progress of services rendered by Pestex Universal."

"But…how was I supposed to know about the sealant??"

Hale shrugged. "I'm sorry, Mister Clart, but contractually the responsibility was yours, whether you knew about the sealant or not. Ignorance is not a defence in this case. But do feel free to consult with a legal expert if you doubt me."

Hale's confident tone didn't leave much room for doubt in Clart's mind. "I…don't have time for that!" he snarled. "Just *fix this!*"

Hale regarded him mildly. "Well, Mister Clart, Pestex is only too happy to offer its services in removing the assassin bugs, but I'm afraid it won't be a *free* service, since we're not liable for any failure of the previous service rendered." He punched up the relevant clause in the contract and showed it to Clart.

Clart ground his teeth for a moment, wondering if he could overcome his biophobia sufficiently to grab Hale around the neck. "All right," he muttered eventually. "Go ahead! Do whatever you have to do! Just *get those creatures out of my kitchen!*"

"With pleasure!" Hale said. "Now, I'll need you to sign an addendum to the original service contract to confirm acceptance of additional services. I'd also highly recommend a further round of psychological modification, to help you cope with the extended—"

"Yes! Alright!" Clart barked. "Let's just do it! But you can bet I'll be looking over the contract very carefully this time…"

"Yeeees…" Hale said slowly, looking around the kitchen. "I can completely understand why you're so upset, Mister Clart."

The fist-sized Tauran amoeboid that had been released under Clart's refrigerator a week earlier had undergone significant changes since Hale had last seen it and was now plastered across every visible kitchen surface as an enormous, gelid layer of pulsating slime that dripped from the walls, counters and fittings.

"You told me that thing would encyst itself in a corner somewhere once it absorbed all the assassin bugs!" Clart raged.

"Hm," Hale said. "Premature onset of the fission cycle. The suppliers assured me that wouldn't happen for another three months. I wonder what brought it on?"

"Don't give me that! You've done it again! Made a complete mess of things! And this time I'm going to sue!"

Hale nodded sympathetically. "Once again, I can understand your frustration, Mister Clart, but I should advise that Pestex can't be held responsible for this."

"Rubbish!" Clart snarled. "Clause eleven of the contract states that Pestex has to disclose any behavioural traits in any organisms used in the course of your services—and I've memorised this next bit—'that may impact the living arrangements of the client beyond any basic inconveniences described and agreed upon in the service contract'!" He gestured angrily towards the throbbing mess. "This is well beyond the inconvenience caused by having one organism destroy another, and I'll be taking legal action over this!"

"I'm glad to hear you've read your contract," Hale said. "However, as I've already mentioned, this is *not* normal behaviour for an amoeboid, and clause *twelve* of the contract states that Pestex shall not be held responsible for any inconvenience caused by *aberrant* behaviour in organisms used in the course of service." He gestured towards the massive slick of slime. "I couldn't tell you why this has occurred, Mister Clart, but I can say that you don't have grounds for legal action."

Clart gritted his teeth. "But…what do I do now? I want that thing removed!"

"Well, we can draw up another addendum to the original contract, so long as you're happy to continue using our services. We wouldn't want to force you into any arrangement you're not happy with, after all. There is one silver lining to all this, though," Hale added.

"Which is??"

"Well, I can see that you're angry about all of this, Mister Clart, and justifiably so. But you don't actually seem especially *phobic*, which means the psychological modification treatments are definitely working."

Clart shot Hale an intensely hateful look.

"I would, however, suggest an additional round of PM, as the organisms we'll be using to clean up the amoeboid are considered…visually triggering by many."

"Hell!" Clart's face paled. "What are they?"

"Arcturan wasps. Not actual insects, I should point out, so the sealant shouldn't impact them at all. But unpleasantly insectoid in appearance, with more teeth and eyes and limbs than you'd think appropriate."

"Fine!" Clart muttered. "Whatever it takes!"

"Well," Hale marvelled as he looked around the kitchen again. "This is…all very impressive!"

Clart smiled tightly. "Isn't it just?" he agreed, in a tone that indicated barely restrained fury. "What happened—and I should tell you that it was the wasps themselves that told me this—is that they've formed an extremely talkative, semi-sentient gestalt entity, and have now transformed my kitchen into the hive-city you see before us, using a mix of chewed-up linoleum and ceiling insulation to create a sort of concrete. They also took a vote to exclude me from the kitchen because my presence was apparently having a negative impact upon their 'vibe'."

"No offence, dude!" a tiny voice buzzed from a nearby burrow.

"At that point I took it upon myself to do a bit of research into the Arcturan wasp, and it seems that *this*," Clart indicated the hive-city again, "is a known aspect of their behaviour. Which means, of course, that I absolutely will be pursuing legal action against Pestex Universal."

Hale nodded sympathetically. "Yes, see, unfortunately you did insist upon us using a greater-than-normal number of the wasps to deal with the amoeboid. Three swarms, in fact. And the contract states very clearly that Pestex takes no responsibility for any issues that arise as a direct result of the client ignoring the recommendations of their Pestex representative."

"What recommendations? You didn't make any recommendations!"

"I certainly did, Mister Clart—I told you that the job would require a single swarm of wasps, but you insisted upon three swarms in order to get the job done faster, and I said that I didn't think that was the best course of action but that I would acquiesce to your wishes."

"But…that wasn't a *recommendation!* That was just something you *said!* And anyway, when I asked you to bring in more wasps, you never mentioned that anything like this could happen!"

"As the on-site expert here, I'm not contractually obliged to tell you what may occur if you don't follow advice, Mister Clart—just to inform you of what the recommended service should achieve. And," Hale added, as Clart opened his mouth to protest further, "if you check your contract a little more carefully, you'll find that exact information listed under clause nineteen."

For a moment Clart looked ready to explode. Then he slumped, seemingly drained of energy. "So…what now? Another addendum to the contract? Another round of PM treatment? More organisms let loose in my kitchen?"

Hale shrugged politely. "Whatever it takes, Mister Clart. Whatever it takes."

"It's the amoeboid all over again!" Clart moaned. He pointed towards the multitude of small, hexagonal crystalline structures dotting the kitchen counter. "Look, it's even growing across the walls and ceilings! *And* the floors! I have to wade through it every time I want to get to my refrigerator!"

"Well, at least the PM is working," Hale noted. "And the Plutonian krystallite did get rid of the wasps."

"Yes—digested them alive!" Clart shuddered. "In the end I had to shove gel plugs into my ears to block out their tiny screams. I know they were never truly sentient, but it was still extremely unpleasant."

Hale shrugged. "Unfortunately death is a constant in the pest control business, Mister Clart." He glanced at kitchen counter. "I'm assuming there was just enough organic detritus covering your kitchen surfaces to allow the krystallite to enter a stage of rapid growth."

"Organic detritus? That's impossible—I've got a J-Seventeen cleaning system!"

"And when was the last time you had it serviced?"

There was a long pause.

"It was due for a service a few weeks ago," Clart finally admitted. "But I forgot all about it. I've never forgotten before! I've never even needed to set an automatic reminder!"

Hale nodded. "Usually your biophobia would keep that sort of thing at the front of your mind, I imagine. But with the success of the PM…" He trailed off. "Which, I'll just point out, Pestex isn't legally responsible for."

"That figures," Clart muttered despondently.

"Well, not to worry. We can fix this easily enough. All we need to do—"

"Look," Clart said tersely, "I'll sign anything, I'll agree to anything, if you can just sterilise my home once and for all! Do you think you can manage that without any more problems, or mistakes, or delays? *Do* you?"

"Most certainly." Hale opened his compendium and pulled up the relevant addendums on the tablet. "Just sign there," he said, proffering the device to Clart. "And there…"

Clart duly pressed his thumb against the relevant spots. "I notice there's no mention here of additional PM."

Hale shook his head. "You won't need it this time." He withdrew a compact, pistol shaped device from the compendium, and glanced at Clart. "You'd best cover your eyes," he cautioned, placing a hand across his own eyes as he pointed the device at the centre of the kitchen floor. "Wide-angle organic scourer—gives off quite a flash."

Clart did as he was told. There was a brief strobing flare of white light, followed by a sharp odour that faded almost immediately. Clart hesitantly opened his eyes, and saw that the krystallite growths had all completely vanished, leaving every kitchen surface looking bright and clean.

"That's it?" Clart asked.

"That's it," Hale affirmed, stowing the scourer away again.

"So…absolutely no further action required?"

"Absolutely none. The infestation has been fully sterilised, Mister Clart."

Clart took a deep breath. "Not that I'm not grateful," he began, in a manner that suggested otherwise, "but couldn't you just have used the scourer to destroy the original infestation of cockroaches?"

Hale shook his head. "Not permitted, I'm afraid, as it's not a natural method of pest control."

Clart narrowed his eyes. "Then…how come you were able to use it on the krystallite?"

"Well, rather fortunately for us, once the krystallite has gone through a cycle of rapid growth, as occurred here, it actually enters a sort of dormant state where it's no longer truly 'alive' in any real sense of the word—no respiration, or consumption, or excretion—merely existing as an inert collection of silicates until it again comes into contact with materials that can fuel its growth, at which point it reanimates, so to speak."

"Well, couldn't you have used the krystallite to destroy the cockroaches, then just zapped the krystallite afterwards?"

Hale shook his head again. "Cockroaches are remarkably resistant to the krystallites' corrosive enzymes."

"I see," Clart said brusquely. "Well, seeing as the job's over now, I'd very much like to just pay my bill and get back to my life, if you wouldn't mind."

Hale nodded agreeably, and began to make a series of calculations on the tablet. "Absolutely, Mister Clart. So, let's see... That's...four service calls, four PM treatments, assassin bugs, Tauran amoeboid, Arcturan wasps—three swarms—Plutonian krystallite. Plus a charge for use of the organic scourer..." He smiled at Clart. "You'll be glad to know, however, that there's also a ten-percent overall discount for repeated use of our service, so..." He completed his calculations and handed the compendium to Clart. "There we go, Mister Clart. If you could just have a quick look over that and authorise transfer of payment..."

Clart's eye's bulged, his face turning crimson. Trembling, he jabbed a finger towards the figure displayed at the bottom of the tablet screen. "Wh-what the *hell* is *this?!*"

"I'm sorry, Mister Clart—is there a problem?"

"Of course there's a damned problem! I can't afford *this!* This is more than I'd make in four standard solar *years!* It's more than the current value of all my combined assets, let alone my savings! How can getting rid of a bunch of damned cockroaches possibly cost *so much??*"

"The fees were clearly listed in the supplemental information package at the back of the contract, Mister Clart. If you'd taken the time to access the link—"

"*I needed to get the job done!*" Clart shouted. "I needed it done *immediately!* I didn't have any damned time to—!" He threw the compendium, tablet and all, to the floor. "There's no way I'm paying this! I absolutely refuse! In fact, I'm...I'm going to *sue* you! Yes! My lawyers will find something to get you on, don't you worry about *that!* And when they do—!"

"The cockroaches are *gone*, Mister Clart," Hale said, his demeanour suddenly cold. He bent to pick up his compendium, then made a show of casually brushing non-existent dust from the cover with his hand. "Which means that, despite the various obstacles and delays encountered along the way—all of which Pestex has been covered for under the terms of the contract, as we've previously discussed—we have absolutely discharged our contractual obligations to you in full. And I can assure you that our corporate lawyers—who, I might add, are among the best and most expensive in all of Human Space—took a great deal of time and care to ensure that our contract templates are, and always will be, utterly airtight upon being signed by the client." He punched up a copy of Clart's contract on the tablet, and held it out for Clart to see. "That *is* your signature, is it not?"

Clart ground his teeth in impotent rage.

"Which means," Hale continued, "that you're bound by the terms and conditions of the contract, according to which you're now obliged to pay in full."

Clart tottered over to his chair and collapsed into it. "But…but I *can't* pay! I genuinely can't *afford* it! I don't *have* that kind of money!"

Hale gave him a pitying look. "Well then, we have a problem, I'm afraid."

Clart buried his face in his hands. "What am I going to do?"

Hale shrugged. "Well, realistically, the only option seems to be that you immediately pay us what you can, and Pestex takes legal action to recover the remainder of the amount owed through liquidation of your assets, and so on."

"Is there…do you not even have some sort of payment plan available?" Clart begged.

Hale considered for a moment. "Well…not as such."

Clart peered through his fingers. "What do you mean, 'not as such'?"

"Well, there *is* a clause in the Pestex franchisee manual…"

Clart jumped to his feet. "Well? Let's hear it!"

Hale hesitated, then nodded. "Okay then." He fished something from one of the inner pockets of the compendium, and quickly tossed it to Clart. "Catch!"

Clart automatically reached out and caught the palm-sized object one-handed—then recoiled.

Encased within the clear plastic disc he held was the ugliest, most ferocious-looking organism he had ever had the misfortune to lay eyes upon. Eight soulless black eyes glared up at Clart from atop a bulbous, black-furred body. Although obviously deceased, the creature radiated an almost tangible aura of menace, all eight legs braced as if ready to spring, glistening fangs poised to sink into soft, yielding flesh.

Clart made a small noise in the back of his throat, clutching the paperweight in a frozen grip.

"The Sydney funnel-web spider," Hale explained. "A relatively small one, from Old Earth."

"I…you…" Clart spluttered.

"Tell me—how do you feel?" Hale asked.

"Wh-what?" With great effort, Clart tore his gaze from the spider and stared at Hale. "*Feel?* What do you mean? I don't—" It suddenly struck him that he didn't really feel *anything*, apart from the sudden shock—now fading—of finding the spider in his hand, and a mild sense of revulsion. Or was it only a memory of the revulsion he *should* have felt? He glared suspiciously at Hale. "I don't understand—what's happened?"

"Well, it seems your PM treatments have been so effective that your biophobia has, for all practical purposes, been *cured*, Mister Clart. Which brings us to the second option for payment of your account."

Clart narrowed his eyes. "Go on…"

"Well, in the event of the client being unable to pay, and in the interests of not having to drag this all out in court, I, as a Pestex Universal franchisee, am authorised to offer the client a three-year apprenticeship, during which time the client—that's you—will work off their outstanding debt while receiving full training, as well as board and other necessities."

There was a long pause.

"You're...offering me a *job?*" Clart asked incredulously.

"It's a good solution. You avoid the legal issues, and Pestex Universal gets a new employee at a time when attracting staff is proving difficult." Hale punched up some information on his tablet and showed it to Clart. "That's the starting wage for a Pestex apprentice. You'd have your debt paid in full within two years."

Clart's eyes bulged.

"The average annual income for a Pestex *franchisee* is almost ten times that figure. Just something to think about in case you consider buying into the business after your apprenticeship." Hale raised an eyebrow. "That is, assuming you accept our offer...?"

Clart thought about it. Then he thought about it some more. Then he nodded slowly. "Okay," he said. "I'm...I'm in, I suppose."

"Excellent!" Hale extended his hand, which Clart grasped without even flinching. "Welcome aboard. I'll get you to read and sign some forms, then you can throw together some clothes and personal belongings, and we'll get you back to the office and start your training right away." He punched up the necessary forms on the tablet and handed the compendium to Clart. "To be honest, I'm actually quite looking forward to finally having some company back at the office."

Clart looked up from the tablet. "So I'm going to be working for *you*, then? Specifically, I mean."

"You don't have a problem with that, I hope?"

There was a short silence, during which Clart narrowed his eyes slightly. "Tell me something," he said eventually. "You've mentioned that it's hard to recruit staff due to widespread social biophobia."

"Yes?"

"Well, it just struck me that Pestex *could* use psychological manipulation as a direct means of recruitment, by eliminating a potential employee's biophobia. Hypothetically, of course."

Hale didn't respond.

"Although," Clart continued, "I'd assume few people would willingly undergo PM, knowing that doing so would make them amenable to being around organisms...unless they had a very good reason to do so, such as needing to be able to deal with Pestex's natural pest control treatments. But even then, there's no reason why anyone would necessarily agree to become a Pestex employee *after* undergoing PM—unless, of course, they had no real *choice* in the matter."

Hale shrugged slightly. "It's certainly an interesting idea."

"Indeed. And it makes me wonder…how did *you* come to be recruited by Pestex, exactly?"

There was a very long pause.

"As a Pestex Universal franchisee," Hale said eventually, "I always find our manual an invaluable resource on how to respond to queries from clients and employees alike, including queries regarding the ways in which the company operates and conducts itself. And so, as per the company manual, my response to both your hypothesis, and your query regarding my recruitment, is simply that Pestex Universal would never—under any circumstances—engage in any activity not legally enforceable through our contracts and internal policies." The brief smile he flashed at Clart didn't quite touch his eyes. "I can assure you, Mister Clart, that there's nothing illegal about Pestex's use of psychological manipulation. Like the assassin bugs, the amoeboid, the wasps, the krystallite, and even the organic scourer, PM is just one of our…tools of the trade."

"Yes," Clart said slowly. "That's what I thought, Mister Hale."

Catfish

The alien spaceship drifted down from the clouds with a soft whine, coming to rest in the middle of the beautifully manicured front lawn of the White House. The President of the United States of America and her sizeable entourage, standing on a hastily-arranged ceremonial carpet a dozen or so metres from the craft, waited nervously as part of the hull slid aside and a metal ramp began to extend smoothly from the resulting gap.

A thousand cell phones, held aloft by a thousand ordinary Americans standing beyond the White House fence, flashed and clicked as a distinctly inhuman figure—sleek and silver-scaled, with a wide, bewhiskered mouth like that of a catfish—wandered casually down the ramp and made its way towards the welcome party.

A few metres from the carpet, the alien being stopped abruptly. It gave the President a hard stare, then opened its mouth as if to speak, hesitated, then closed its mouth again. After a moment it held up a fin-like hand as if requesting a moment, and began rummaging inside the flat, metallic-looking carry bag slung over its shoulder.

The President turned to glance at her closest advisor, who shrugged, then leaned closer to suggest that the President move forward with her welcome speech.

The President nodded stiffly, turning back to the piscine alien visitor and smiling warmly as she raised a hand in what one of her staff members—a rabid Trekkie—had assured her would be instantly recognisable as a gesture of peace and welcome. "On behalf of all the peoples and nations of planet Earth," she began, "as the President of these United States of America, it deeply honours me to welcome you to—"

"Wait," the alien interrupted. "Just…look, I'm really sorry, but—" Withdrawing its fin from the bag, it held aloft a metallic object. "Did *you* send this out?"

The President regarded the twelve-inch gold-coloured disc the alien was holding. Something about the disc tugged at her memory…

An advisor slipped in behind the President and whispered urgently in her ear, "That's the Voyager disc! We sent a copy of that thing out on each of the two Voyager probes in nineteen seventy-seven!"

The President made no comment, continuing to smile as the alien stared at her. "Ah, yes. I believe so," she said eventually. "Is there an issue?"

The alien gave her a hard stare. "There certainly is!" It turned the disc around to show the President the naked, stylised human figures inscribed on the back.

"You," the alien griped, glaring at the President of the United States of America, "look absolutely *nothing* like your profile pic!"

Andromeda Spaceways Pre-Booking Guide

Thank you…

…for considering the services of **Andromeda Spaceways™** for your next intergalactic voyage.

To ensure the legal, financial and physical wellbeing of **Andromeda Spaceways™** and its passengers, we ask all prospective customers to study this handy guide carefully before making a booking. **Andromeda Spaceways™** take no responsibility for passengers' ignorance of any of the rules and guidelines listed herein.

We hope that you will choose to fly with us, and we greatly look forward* to your custom.

* With regards to Time-Travellers and Chrononauts, we also look backward to your custom.

Conditions of Carriage (Priority*)

1. **Andromeda Spaceways™** accepts all forms of legal tender—with the exception of **Credits**, due to recent fluctuations on the Intergalactic Currency Market—as payment for fares and other

services. Please note that Time-Travellers are required to make all payments in cash.

2. Multiple cloned individuals travelling together will not qualify for discount family rates on fares. Multiple clones are also not permitted to book single seats with the intention of 'time-sharing,' and must secure and pay for one seat per physical individual.

3. Sentient viruses and other microscopics are permitted to book as a single passenger if inhabiting the body of a single larger sentient individual. Please note that the legal limit for microscopic passengers per carrier is 653 billion. Given the identical genetic inheritance of most individuals within a swarm, groups in excess of 653 billion will qualify for discount family rates on bookings for two or more carriers. The booking of non-sentient carriers into passenger berths is not permitted.

4. Bookings and payments for **Andromeda Spaceways™** flights in dimensions or realities parallel to Prime, or in alternate timelines, will not be considered valid in the Prime dimension, reality, or timeline.

5. Passengers with powers of teleportation requiring passage only to within teleportation range of their destination will still be obliged to pay full fare.

6. Passengers with mind-reading abilities…well, you know.

7. In the unlikely event of any **Andromeda Spaceways™** flight becoming trapped in a temporary Causality Loop, passengers will not incur any additional payments for repetition of services.

8. In the unlikely event of any **Andromeda Spaceways™** flight becoming trapped in a temporary Causality Loop, passengers will not incur any additional payments for repetition of services.

9. In any situation where **Andromeda Spaceways™** flights reach relativistic speeds, **Andromeda Spaceways™** absolves itself of any responsibility for the effects of time-dilation upon the personal, cultural, or financial status of its passengers.

* For a full and detailed listing of all **Andromeda Spaceways™** Conditions of Carriage, a handy 10,000 page guide can be downloaded from our server.

Dangerous Goods—Travelling safely

The following items are not permitted aboard **Andromeda Spaceways™** flights as either checked or cabin baggage:

a) Explosives, Fireworks and Incendiary Devices.
b) Flammable or Inflammable liquids.
c) Illegal narcotics.
d) Weapons of any variety, except upon religious grounds, which must be declared and authorised prior to departure.
e) Vegemite (see Weapons).
f) Other sentient beings.
g) Pocket universes, miniature black holes, or other unstable phenomena.
h) Wibbles.
i) Audio recordings of Freestyle Jazz (due to their effect upon crystalline passengers).

Baggage Restrictions

Allowances for Checked Baggage vary depending upon the dimensional transcendentalism of the craft being utilised for each specific flight. Please consult the schematics listed for each **Andromeda Spaceways™** flight prior to completing any booking.

Cabin baggage is restricted to the following per passenger:

a) One medium-sized carry bag or briefcase.
b) One medium-sized backpack.
c) Two additional small digestive tracts.
d) Four medium-sized removable appendages (cybernetic or organic).

Code of Conduct

Our inflight staff strive to provide the best in customer service at all times. If, however, you are unhappy with any aspect of our inflight customer service program, please refer the matter to our 500kg Andromedan **Complaints Officer*** immediately.

1. All cabin baggage must be stored either under the seat in front of you or in the overhead lockers.
2. Mobile electronic communication devices, mystical icons, and telekinetic abilities should be deactivated prior to and during flight as these may interfere with navigational equipment.
3. Seatbelts must be worn at all times while the **Fasten Seatbelt** sign is lit. Passengers may release their seatbelts when the sign is no longer lit. Passengers on flights without artificial gravity are advised to keep their seatbelts fastened at all times.
4. The consumption of nutritive materials brought aboard by passengers is not permitted during flights.
5. The consumption of **Andromeda Spaceways™** foods or beverages in the onboard restrooms while in flight is not permitted.
6. The consumption of other passengers while in flight is not permitted, except upon religious grounds, which must be declared and authorised prior to departure.
7. The consumption of other passengers in the onboard restrooms while in flight is not permitted at any time.
8. Smoking, garfling, f'nargling, and other carcinogenic activities are not permitted aboard **Andromeda Spaceways™** flights.
9. Passengers composed of pure energy, or with pyrokinetic abilities, are requested to restrict combustive activities to the restrooms, except where such restrooms are being utilised by gaseous passengers.
10. Acts of terrorism will not be tolerated aboard any **Andromeda Spaceways™** flight, except upon religious grounds, which must be declared and authorised prior to departure.

11. Acts of sexual congress in the passenger berth are not permitted, except upon religious grounds or instinctive biological imperatives, which must be declared and authorised prior to departure.

12. Passengers who reproduce via cellular fission will be expected to pay in full for the seating of any progeny produced during the flight, except where such reproduction is shown to be an instinctive biological imperative, which must be declared and authorised prior to departure.

Note: Passengers who violate any of the codes of conduct listed above will be ejected from the ship at the nearest port-of-call. In the event of code violation aboard a non-stop flight, **Andromeda Spaceways™** reserves the right to take appropriate action, up to and including ejection of the offender into open vacuum, or travelling back in time to shoot the offender's grandfather.

* **Andromeda Spaceways™** accepts no responsibility for physical injuries resulting from complaints made to our **Complaints Officer.**

Emergency Protocols

In the event of an **Emergency Situation** aboard any **Andromeda Spaceways™**, the following will occur:

1. Breathing masks will automatically fall from the locker above your cranial organ. Non-oxygen breathers should make themselves known to staff prior to departure. To activate breathing masks, simply pull down and place the cup over your respiratory organ(s). Passengers possessing multiple respiratory organs should make themselves known to staff prior to departure. If travelling with immature offspring, please secure your own mask before attending to your young. Passengers with automatic predatory panic-reflexes should devour their young before securing masks.

2. Emergency lights will indicate the route from your seat to the nearest **Emergency Locker**. Please make your way calmly to your designated locker, which will contain one **Deep Space Evac Survival Suit** per passenger*. **Special Needs passengers** (i.e. those possessing more than one head or body) should make their specific needs known when booking.

3. To put on your suit, simply put on your suit. Respiratory gasses will immediately be released from the tank behind your helmet(s)*. Surviving **Andromeda Spaceways™** staff will then direct you to the nearest escape pod.

4. Please note that **Andromeda Spaceways™** flights are equipped with sufficient escape pods for all **First Class passengers***. Each pod is equipped with:

   a. A distress beacon, with a battery half-life of 5,000 standard galactic years;

   b. Provisions enough to sustain up to six passengers of various species for a period of 1.6 standard hours;

   c. Multispecies first-aid supplies;

   d. Pornographic literature, to assist in passing the long hours before death or rescue;

   e. **Do-It-Yourself Euthanasia Kits**, compatible with most body chemistries, which include **Legal Will Kits**, various religious icons and texts, and lightweight body-bags.

5. In the event of planetfall, each pod is equipped with a whistle, which crash survivors can use to either draw attention to their position or amuse themselves.

6. In the event of rescue, survivors will accept as a condition of booking that **Andromeda Spaceways™** is legally absolved of any and all perceived negligence contributing to or directly resulting in any emergency situation arising aboard any **Andromeda Spaceways™** flight. As a gesture of good faith, rescued survivors will be eligible for a refund of exactly half the cost of their fare* (Conditions Apply).

* Except on **Budget Flights**.

Note: Andromeda Spaceways™ are justifiably proud of their safety record. The likelihood of any **Andromeda Spaceways™** flight encountering a major emergency situation is a mere .001%. However, in the unlikely event of a crash or hull breach, death is 99% certain.

Thank You...
...for taking the time to read this **Pre-Booking Guide**. We hope that it will assist you in choosing to make **Andromeda Spaceways™** *your* preferred interstellar carrier, whether you travel for the purposes of business, pleasure, spawning, or conquest.

For Further Enquiries
Please call the toll-free, easy-to-remember **Andromeda Spaceways™** comms number:

(05947##)
53246532947037473254932175987594375843273 74—
574223757435874375743574574757435872745735 4—
784325457437574375794757487584795749757457 4—
397457437574375437527543209437529437504750 9—
743550845320957094375975943759487597439574 39—
5743759747594375
Extension: 01

Old Habits Die

Jed sat on his porch, glaring out at the thick jungle that covered the entire surface of Venus, fondling the stock of his ancient laser-rifle.

"Dammit!" he spat. "Haven't spotted one damn *shmeerp* all day! The only decent food-animal on this entire God-forsaken hellhole of a planet, especially now that cows and pigs are extinct on Earth—and even if they weren't, they'd be too damned expensive to import! So we settlers have to depend on *shmeerp* meat, which would be fine, if there were any damn *shmeerps* around!" He turned to Zev, standing beside him. Zev was only a clone, not a *real* person, but Jed enjoyed venting his frustrations to his servant. "Am I right?"

"Yes, Master," Zev agreed. He had no real opinion on the way in which Jed insisted they both speak, which—Jed had once told him—was a throwback to a time following the great Social Media Expansion, where misunderstandings over the true meaning of abbreviated and stylised communications had led to wars, and worse. Conversation without full exposition, Jed opined, opened the participants up to potentially not being privy to vital information. And on Venus, this could well prove deadly. "I have seen no *shmeerp* for nearly two *klaan*,"

Zev went on. "Perhaps you should go hunting for Spiderworms instead, as their flesh is delicious."

Jed blanched. "You know as well as I do that Spiderworms are the fiercest beasts on Venus! You'll not catch *me* hunting them! Better to starve, which we may do if the *shmeerp* population doesn't increase. Damned Global Space Corp—this is all *their* fault! By increasing the cost of imports they force us to live off the land, while they destroy the native wildlife with their incessant mining, so we end up having to work for *them* in order to buy food, working harder and harder for pitiful pay, until we're forced to quit, only to sink deeper into poverty, so we have to beg for our jobs back at a fraction of our original pay!"

Zev remained quiet. He knew all of this, but—as always—it was better to be exposed to these truths over and over again than for Jed to risk omitting any detail that Zev was not already privy to. Besides which, Jed was clearly on a roll.

"Dammit," Jed continued, "the Global Space Corp *own* us, and want to dictate everything we do—even the way we think and talk! 'New, efficient speech patterns' they say. 'Better for productivity.' 'Clipped dialogue' and 'basic information only.' *Pah!* What's wrong with the old way of speaking? Exposition, and lots of it! How else can a person understand the *nature* of what's being discussed? If the GSC gets its way, no longer will a man be able to enjoy a deep and involving conversation with his friends! No longer will he be able to dwell upon important aspects of the past, so that others will understand *exactly* the meaning of his words. And do you know what they've based this ridiculous coda upon?" He glared at Zev. "The ramblings of Old-Time *science-fiction writers!* 'Show, don't tell' they used to say, and the GSC blindly followed their bidding! How is man supposed to live by such ridiculous rules, especially here on Venus?"

Unfortunately, the Spiderworm that had been attracted by Jed's incessant chatter chose that very moment to pounce, and Jed—distracted by his own monologue—never even had time to raise his rifle.

Too late, Jed realised that minimal exposition had certain advantages…

With a start, Jed sat up in his chair. It had all been a dream! Thank God!

There was a sudden growl from the jungle.

As the Spiderworm leapt towards him, Jed realised that this was no dream after all…

Customer Service

The Oncarri were nightmarish to look at. Fortunately, they were also superb linguists.

"Which is bloody handy," the Oncarri Emissary opined in a slow, ocker drawl. "Using your own communication platforms to chat to you in the local lingo before putting in a personal appearance sure as hell went a long way towards everyone calming the eff down, don't you reckon? Otherwise you'd've tried to nuke us the second we showed our faces."

The Australian Prime Minister smiled nervously, leaning back in the ornate chair behind his antique jarrah desk. "Look, I can understand how you might get that impression from our media, but I like to think we Aussies are a little more hospitable than, say, the Americans. Probably a good thing you landed on our lawn instead of in front of the White House."

The Emissary smiled back, which just looked terrifying coming from a being resembling a gigantic mutant scorpion. "No offence, mate, but we've done our research, and the typical response by any human anywhere to anything scary-looking has always been to hit it with a stick. That's nothing to be embarrassed about, mind you. Completely instinctive. You couldn't fight it even if you wanted to."

The Prime Minister's smile tightened slightly. "Well…I do hope we're not going to allow assumptions and 'what if's' to distract from what seems to have been a very peaceful First Contact situation."

The Emissary sighed. "No assumptions. Just facts." It held up four of its hands in a placatory gesture. "Sorry, look, to be blunt, the Oncarri prefer to cut through all the bullshit straight away when meeting new races. That way, everyone knows where they stand. No nasty surprises."

"That's…fair enough, I suppose."

"Right? Not gonna lie, along with our gift of the gab, the 'no bullshit' approach is one of the reasons we're so successful at interspecies communication. It all helps with First Contact situations, as well as with selling our commercial services."

The Prime Minister raised an eyebrow. "Commercial services?"

"Yeah, well, I don't wanna sound like we're up ourselves, but the Oncarri are actually the top provider of GM services in this quadrant of the galaxy. Genetic Manipulation," the Emissary added, noting the Prime Minister's blank expression.

The Prime Minister took a moment to mentally flick through the reams of useless trivia he'd accumulated over years of being forced to meet with scientists for photo opportunities. "Genetic Manipulation? So…gene-splicing? Creating new breeds of organism, that sort of thing?"

The Emissary nodded. "Exactly! Also the eradication of genetic illnesses, planetary restructuring—what you'd call 'terraforming'— and a bunch of other stuff. Our biggest sources of revenue are our genetic pest-control programs, which is actually something I thought you might be interested in discussing at some point in the future."

"Oh?"

"Well, I thought—" The Emissary stopped abruptly, and shook its head. "Ah, geez. Sorry, I'm getting ahead of myself. It's my worst habit. My nestmate always says I talk about work too much. And we haven't even signed any treaties yet, let alone talked about the bigger issues—"

"No, no, don't apologise," the Prime Minister interjected. "I mean…talking about business matters is as much a part of us getting to know one another as anything else, don't you think?"

The Emissary leaned back on its haunches. "Huh. I never thought of it like that. That's pretty good. Might have to pinch that line to use on future clients."

The Prime Minister beamed. "Right? So…why did you think we'd be especially interested in your pest control program?"

The Emissary hesitated for a moment, then shrugged agreeably. "Well, for starters, cane toads."

"Cane toads?"

"Nasty little buggers. Valuable part of their native environment, but a real pain in the cloaca for Australians. No natural predators, so they breed unchecked, destroy the native wildlife, and end up costing taxpayers a mint as your government implements one expensively useless eradication scheme after another." The Emissary waved a claw dismissively. "But you know all that already, I assume. Especially with you being a Queensland boy."

"Well, yes. But go on."

"Well, invasive species are a universal problem, and I use that term advisedly. Anytime any species anywhere manages to invade a foreign environment, whether on the same planet or extraterrestrial, the potential for harm can be enormous, which is why our pest control services are always in demand. Plus, if we can't guarantee one-hundred percent success with any given program, we don't undertake the service."

"So you think you could definitely help us with the cane toads?"

The Emissary nodded enthusiastically. "Absolutely! At a glance, I reckon resolving your issue would be just about the easiest operation we could possibly undertake. All it needs is one of our patented programmable viruses, and we'd have your invasive toad population wiped out in no time at all, and without any harm to the local environment. Plus, we can program the virus to remain active indefinitely, thus preventing future incursions."

"Sounds…positive," the Prime Minister admitted. "I'm not sure the folks at Environmental Protection Australia would go for it, though. If the virus got back to the native toad population in North America—"

"Wouldn't happen. The virus'd be programmed to survive within a very limited environmental range. Move it outside the target ecosystem and it kicks the bucket."

"Expensive?"

The Emissary named a figure which brought the Prime Minister out in a cold sweat. "Payable in natural resources."

"Bloody hell!"

"I mean, if you do your sums," the Emissary drawled, "you'll find the expense of the program is about half what your economy'll lose over the next twenty years if you *don't* get rid of the cane toads. Plus, we don't charge subscriptions or residuals. One fee, paid once, with a lifetime guarantee on the continuing effectiveness of the program."

The Prime Minister snorted. "My lifetime or yours?"

"Earth's."

"Oh."

"And obviously we can apply the same program to other invasive species such as hornets, black rats, elm leaf beetles, sea-stars, camphor trees, foxes, mosquito fish, African boxthorn, and numerous species of wasp and ant. We can even tweak viruses to attack feral populations of rabbits, pigs, goats, camels, cats, water buffaloes, trout, carp, and so on, without affecting domestic stock." The Emissary grinned horribly. "Clever, eh?"

"You've…certainly done your research."

"Of course. Another reason why we're the best at what we do."

The Prime Minister nodded thoughtfully. "Well…I'll have to run it through Senate, of course, but…I'm pretty sure we can do business. Perhaps we could schedule another meeting to discuss details? Say, Tuesday, over lunch?"

The Emissary consulted an electronic device strapped to one of its many wrists. "Yeah, well, I can fit you in. But, just to let you know, I *do* have appointments scheduled with a couple of other potential clients *prior* to Tuesday, so if you want to actually book a service you'll need to jump in quickly so they don't book before you do."

The Prime Minister frowned. "You already have other appointments? And why is it an issue to wait on making a booking?"

"Well, we've been here almost three weeks, so I've had plenty of opportunity to get out and about and chat to people, and even attend some meetings already. Not all of them were business related, of course, but some look like they'll lead to firm bookings." The Emissary noted the Prime Minister's sour expression. "Some humans prefer to get straight down to business, find out what we have to offer, discuss services—which obviously I do, as any good business representative would—rather than spend weeks consulting with colleagues, committees and caterers on what sort of shindig they should throw for a visiting alien emissary. As for why you need to book asap," the Emissary leaned forward, "our service policy is 'first come, first served,' and we only service one customer at a time—per planet, that is. The upside of this is that we can give each job our complete and undivided attention. The downside is we sometimes end up with a backlog of customers on a given planet, all waiting their turn. If you don't book now you could be waiting a while, depending upon how long the queue gets." It sat back and waited expectantly.

The Prime Minister hesitated, then nodded firmly. "Okay, okay, I'm in. The Senate won't be happy, and the Opposition'll be ropeable, but I'll just have to impress upon them the need to move on this."

The Emissary beamed. "Great! So, just the cane toads for now, or…?"

"Yes, I think so. Once the toads are gone, every lefty and greenie in Australia will want to poke around to make sure we haven't stuffed up, and hopefully by the time they're through you'll have a window in your schedule to fit us in again."

"Sure. I mean, there may be a bit of a wait, but we're not going anywhere while there's still demand for our services, so…"

"Okay then." The Prime Minister stood and grasped one of the Emissary's appendages, shaking it warmly. "Where do I sign?"

Just three months on, it was all over. For the cane toads, at least.

"The EPA's been scouring the entire country for the past month," the Prime Minister. "Haven't found a single living cane toad, adult, tadpole or egg. The Greens are singing our praises for the first time in living history, and our approval ratings are the highest ever!"

"Glad to hear it," the Emissary said. "I s'pose that means you'll retain office long enough for us to do business again?"

"Absolutely!" The Prime Minister rubbed his hands together. "So. Do you have room in your busy schedule for us to meet and discuss booking in another round of pest control?"

The Emissary consulted the device on its wrist. "I could do…the first Monday in December? Noon?"

"Done."

"Excellent. I'll have to make tracks for now, though. Got a meeting with our next client."

The Prime Minister held up his hands. "Yes, of course, I completely understand. The Americans must be getting impatient." He grinned. "Probably a new experience for them, having to wait in line. Be sure to offer my apologies for monopolising your time."

The Emissary regarded him oddly. "Yeah. I'll be sure to do that. When I meet 'em."

The true significance of that last comment went straight over the Prime Minister's head.

"You again honour this *warrangan* one with your invitation to *girinyalanha*."

Bijaa nodded, appreciating the Emissary's courtesy in speaking Wiradjuri. "I hear you just had a meeting upstairs in the Prime Minister's office."

The Emissary shrugged. "It was hardly a secret. Nor was the information discussed, particularly."

"Cane toads?

"Indeed. But had the Prime Minister insisted, I can assure you that I would have taken steps to ensure the absolute secrecy of that meeting, along with engaging the same anti-eavesdropping protocols I'm applying as we speak," the Emissary indicated its wrist device, "as requested by you at our last meeting. We do take client directives very seriously, you know."

"Oh, I wasn't—"

"No bullshitting, *malayarr*. Our linguistic skills extend to extrapolating the probable flow of discussions. Yet another reason the Oncarri are so good at interspecies communication."

The elderly Indigenous Australian fingered his tie uncomfortably. "I'm sorry. I wasn't trying to insult your professionalism. It's just that if word of this matter got out…"

"Perhaps that's our cue to get to business?" The Emissary tapped a claw against Bijaa's desk. "So, I assume you've made a decision on whether to commit to booking in the service we discussed previously?"

Biijaa nodded slowly. "Yes. I mean, yes, we want to book it in."

"Excellent. Well, in that case, the Oncarri would be honoured to undertake this task for the National Indigenous Australians Agency."

Bijaa exhaled noisily and slumped in his chair. "I'd thought perhaps you might have…moral objections."

The Emissary nodded understandingly. "We make no judgements upon the ethics of client races. It's bad for business."

"And you can fully comply with all the specifics?"

"Oh, yes. We can absolutely guarantee clearance from just this one continent."

Bijaa dropped his gaze to the desktop. "Good. That's good," he murmured. "We're not hypocrites, you know. We don't want to eliminate the Whitefellas in their *own* lands."

"Of course. And we can also guarantee the virus will be quick-acting and painless. If you truly insist."

Bijaa chewed his lip reflectively. "We'll give 'em every chance to leave beforehand. There'll be a press release, an ultimatum, a deadline to leave. But I reckon most'll think it's some sort of joke, or bluff, or something they can fight. A lot of 'em are gonna die…"

The Emissary coughed politely. "If we could discuss terms of payment?"

Bijaa blinked. "Oh. Yeah. Right. We can give your people access to major unmined uranium deposits on First Nations lands. Afterwards, we can allow access to other sites, if need be. You'll have to make your own arrangements to dig it out, though."

"Perfectly acceptable," the Emissary said, "although the extra effort on our part will bump up the price by five percent."

"I understand."

"Well, then. Shall we make this an official contract?"

Bijaa frowned unhappily. "I wasn't in favour of all this, you know. But majority rules in the NIAA…"

"I *am* due to meet with another client shortly to confirm a booking," pressed the Emissary. "Shall I tell them I have a prior commitment, or…?"

"Very well." Bijaa bowed his head. "May Baiame judge our decision kindly…"

After leaving Bijaa's office, the Emissary scuttled down the hall to the coffee dispenser and dialled itself a hot chocolate. Sipping daintily, it glanced around to ensure it was alone, then pulled the dispenser out from the wall and peered behind it.

"Broodmother Ektar of the Swarm of Hoothis, I presume?"

The cockroach waved its antennae.

"An honour." The Emissary bowed politely. "We received your service request and specifications, and I'm pleased to say the Oncarri would be honoured to undertake the task."

It squatted down on its haunches and regarded its client intently. "So, let me give you some options for dealing with this vertebrate infestation of yours…"

Tragedy

SUPERHERO DIES IN TRAGIC ACCIDENT

Metro City's most popular crimefighter, Mr George Papadopoulos—
better known as 'Captain Invisible'—has died after being struck by a
4WD vehicle late last night. The driver of the 4WD was quoted as
saying that he simply never saw the victim.

Wiping the Smile Off

The plan was simple: infiltrate Earthly society disguised as chartered accountants, and conquer from within. Unfortunately for the shape-shifting Sirian Coprophages, humanity soon learned to identify the invaders; singling out the individuals who seemed a little too pleased with themselves. The ones with the shit-eating grins.

All I Want For Christmas

With a soft pop of burnt air, Sneet reconstituted in a small, rank-smelling cubicle in a room at the back of the building and found themself sitting in the lap of a rotund, white-bearded, middle-aged human male dressed in a crimson suit almost identical to Sneet's own, clutching a half-full bottle of fluid, with his pants around his ankles. Before the human could cry out, Sneet cocooned him, catching the bottle as it fell. The cocoon writhed on the floor for a moment until the sedatives kicked in. Sneet nodded, then sniffed the open top of the bottle and recoiled.

fermented sugars, their implant whispered. *utilised locally as a beverage, as well as an industrial solvent and fuel*

<Frek! Is it lethal?>

eventually

<Why was this information not included in the cerebral download?>

omissions are inevitable—a note has been uploaded to central

"Hoy! Stan!"

Sneet looked up. A small, frustrated-looking human male wearing a white shirt with a black tie and slacks stood in the cubicle doorway. The badge pinned to his breast read: HI, MY NAME IS JEREMY. "Just what the heck—?" His expression changed to one of surprise. "Oh, sorry, I thought—I saw you standing there in your Santa suit and just assumed you were Stan, using the loo without closing the door. As usual. Er...do you happen to know where I can find Stan? I was sure I spotted him sneaking in here." He spied the bottle in Sneet's hand. "I certainly hope that's not what I think it is!"

"It is—" Sneet regarded the label on the bottle, "Clan MacGregor Blended Scotch Whiskey, Product of Scotland. But," they added, noting Jeremy's expression, "it does not belong to me."

Jeremy's shoulders slumped. "Well, I suppose I shouldn't be surprised. So where on earth *is* Stan? Any idea?"

"Not here." *Too obvious?* "He went...outside. Of this building." Sneet performed a quick sift through the cultural lexicon downloaded to their cortex. "To have a smoke."

"But...I didn't see him leave the bathroom."

Sneet performed another sift. "He...went out of the window." They pointed towards the small half-open aperture at the top of the wall at the back of the cubicle.

Jeremy's lip curled. "Again? Frankly, it's hard to reconcile his apparent skills in parkour with the fact that he's seldom able to walk in a straight line after lunch." He glanced at the bottle again. "I'm rather surprised we didn't hear an explosion when he lit his cigarette. Unless that's still to come." His eyes narrowed. "What on earth is *that?*"

Sneet followed Jeremy's gaze. *Frek! The cocoon!* Beneath their human disguise, spinnerets tensed, preparing to spray.

"Good Lord!" Jeremy shook his head despairingly. "What *is* this, a gosh-darned *squat?* Cigarettes, alcohol, and now a *beanbag?* Let me tell you, if we weren't so gosh-darned busy, and the agency wasn't so short on Santas this year—" He paused. "You *are* from the agency, I presume?"

Earlier…

Screaming. Flashes of laser-fire. Boiling mud explodes around them. G'norr soldiers fly backwards, reduced to gobbets of seared flesh. The metallic odours of copper and burnt chitin flavour the air. Greasy smoke rolls across the front, lending cover to the fungoid horrors stampeding towards them. Crouching low, Sneet glares down the sights of their maser, squeezing off precise shots as fleeting gaps in the smoke reveal glimpses of teeth and claws and the diabolical glow of atomic weaponry. Enemy combatants burst like microwaved optics, the survivors rapidly closing the gap between the two opposing forces. Sneet switches their maser to a sustained beam and rakes it across the oncoming horde, flaying tissue from cartilage, until the battery drains and dies. Dropping the weapon, Sneet stands and unsheathes the long razorglass blade at their waist as the slathering monsters bear down upon the remaining g'norr troops—

"Well??"

Sneet blinked. "I—apologies, Fleetlord. Could you repeat, please?" The screams of dying soldiers still echoed in their hindbrain.

Kevlaar fixed Sneet with a cold stare. "I *said*…you will accept the mission?" It was barely a question; more a traditional invitation to comply.

Sneet glanced at the light-up display on the conference table in front of them. "Operation Santa?"

Kevlaar waited expectantly.

Refuse! a tiny voice in Sneet's hindbrain whispered. *You are no longer a soldier. You are a farmer. This will take you away from skutcharvest, and if you are not there to oversee the skuttering—*

Unthinkable! interrupted the part of Sneet's mind forged by race and duty and fire. *Refusal is never an option!*

—the smell of burning bodies clogs their olfactory pits—

Frek!

158

It was being back in this damned place that was causing the flashbacks, Sneet thought; the cold metal underfoot, the overbearing self-importance of military leadership, all awakening the old soldier within. Reactivating the loyal drone. Reviving memories of battle and brutality and bloodshed that Sneet had long kept repressed simply to be able to function post-service.

Hating themself, Sneet bowed their cranium, taking the opportunity to scan the mission specifications. It was the most basic outline they had ever seen, little more than broad planetary specs and a brief explanation of mission goals. *Why me?* they wondered bitterly. *Dragged from retirement, right in the middle of the most important season of the solar cycle! Surely they have mega-legions of younger, faster, more capable operatives available? They must, at the very least, have plenty of less damaged candidates than I...* "Of course, Fleetlord. I...accept." They hesitated. "But, with the greatest respect, a minor query?"

Kevlaar nodded impatiently, leaning back in their web at the other end of the table. "Anticipated. No, you are not being recommissioned. For the purposes of this mission, you shall remain a 'civilian volunteer.' You will, however, be compensated for your input."

A clawshake from one of the minor Systemlords, in other words, Sneet thought sourly. *And not at all what I was wondering...*

"Now," Kevlaar continued, pointing a claw towards Sneet's display, "you will note this incursion does not follow standard procedure." They paused. "I do not suppose *you* can recall the last time that occurred?"

Sneet made a gesture to indicate they could not, skimming over the specs as they scrolled down their display. A *non-military* incursion? What did that even *mean?* How could subjugation of the indigenous population—reportedly still reliant upon fossil fuels, and indulging in intraspecies warfare—require anything other than an armed invasion when—

Sneet blinked in confusion. "Apologies Fleetlord, but...a Level *Three* civilisation? Surely not?"

Kevlaar nodded slowly. "Confirmed by Central. The indigenes *should* qualify as mere animals. Yet these particular animals have somehow developed atomic and wireless technologies, and even primitive spaceflight, hence the seemingly undeserved classification. Indeed, their technology is broadly compatible with our own, and their existing infrastructure can easily be adapted to our requirements, all of which offers a monumental saving of time, effort and finances—and which, frustratingly, is why we cannot simply obliterate this civilisation from orbit. Furthermore, while we outclass these wretched primates in most respects, our surface-level offensive capabilities are far too closely matched for comfort, which is why a military incursion is out of the question..." They trailed off, glaring at their own display.

There was a short silence, as Sneet considered how to frame their next query in a sufficiently respectful manner. "Begging your pardon, Fleetlord," they said eventually, "but—with the very greatest respect— even taking into account the value of the local infrastructure, why would Central seek to claim this world in the face of such inconvenience?"

Kevlaar pointed again towards Sneet's display. "Subsection five."

Sneet scrolled down to the specified information, then reluctantly nodded their understanding. This world was cited as being ideally and uniquely placed to become the primary forward operations base to facilitate expansion into this entire quadrant of the galaxy, and was thus unarguably vital to the ongoing advancement of the G'norr Dominion. But with such staggering complications preventing the use of standard protocols, how—?

Sneet scrolled further. "Apologies, Fleetlord, but I am not familiar with the incursion protocol cited here."

Kevlaar nodded.

"Unsurprising. The 'Deity' protocol has not been employed for many hundreds of cycles. It is an exercise in theatrical nonsense, in my opinion, but has proven successful when required, according to military records. However, to add yet another inconvenience to the list, in this instance we are unable to action the protocol as it currently exists because these primates follow so many distinct and divergent ideologies, with each aggressively opposed to the others, that it completely undermines our ability to infiltrate and conquer by masquerading as a single local deity. This is also why we are unable to impose mass cerebral reprogramming from orbit: the locals are simply too *individualistic*. And setting up full-sized reprogrammers at ground level is out, as local forces would undoubtedly engage long before activation would be possible. Thus, the process must be applied in person, one on one."

One on one??

Sneet opened their mouth to express disbelief. Kevlaar gave them a look. Sneet shut their mouth.

"The extreme value of the planet demands this level of effort," Kevlaar declared. "To this end, operatives will each be equipped with newly-developed, miniaturised cerebral reprogrammers—re-education units—which Central assures us are fully suited to the extreme restrictions of the mission, despite their correspondingly reduced capacity."

Schematics for the REUs flashed up on Sneet's display. *Will these units even be able to tap into the Ego of a species still so developmentally close to being Id-driven animals?* Sneet wondered. *Surely they will simply shake off the effects of the algorithm as easily as any dumb beast would!*

They read on as further information scrolled across the display.

What? WHAT??

'Given the reduced capacity of the REUs, each indigenous subject will require additional personalised reinforcement and embedding of subliminal directives by the supervising operative via cerebral link to their REU, to suit the inferred requirements of the individual subject.'

Frek! Sneet thought incredulously. *But that will take—!*

'Completion of mission estimated at twenty-five local solar cycles.'

FREK!! A full-scale physical military takeover would probably take less than a single cycle!

Kevlaar shot Sneet a look that seemed almost sympathetic. "Be assured, I have expressed to Central my doubts regarding the information you have just noted. But I have been *reminded* that all previously encountered Level Three civilisations were securely bound by the rationality of Ego rather than by the animalistic Id, so even these downsized processors will be able to access the higher cerebral functions of the indigenes."

Sneet nodded unhappily.

"All these obstacles aside," Kevlaar continued, "there is one small ray of starlight peering out from behind the eclipse. The sub-deity for which the operation has been named holds ideological significance for almost forty-five per cent of the indigenous population, and younglings of that percentage are indoctrinated into this ideology also, primarily as a means of behavioural control, which our incursion takes full advantage of."

Sneet nodded again, then hesitated.

"Yes?" Kevlaar asked tersely.

Sneet cringed slightly. "Humblest apologies, Fleetlord. Please know that I intend no disrespect with this query but—honoured though I am to have been considered for this mission—"

"For Freksake! Out with it!"

Sneet took a deep breath. "Well, Fleetlord...I cannot help but wonder...*why?* Specifically, why *me?* That is," they added hastily, "to speak plainly—and I am sure my military records will support me on this—I was never promoted to any rank beyond squadleader, and I cannot imagine that my combat experience lends itself to covert operations of this type. Additionally, I was retired from service a *very* long time ago, so—"

"I agree," Kevlaar interrupted.

There was a long silence.

"I have also looked over the psychological evaluations from your time in service, as well as your ongoing post-discharge assessments."

Another silence.

"There was a time, deep in our past, when veterans with such levels of post-combat neurosis would have been euthanised to minimise risk to society. However, Central, in their infinite wisdom, considers you an essential addition to this operation...despite your involvement being another aspect of the mission about which I have raised concerns. They have, in fact, described you as—" Kevlaar consulted their display again, "—an 'instinctive incursion specialist' owing to your 'highly developed empathic and learning abilities,' placing you in the highest percentile of surviving military personnel with regards to your ability to negotiate unfamiliar environments and interspecies communication. Put simply, Central views you as the best of the best, with the numerous commendations, promotions and career opportunities offered to you during and since your service cited as supporting evidence."

Kevlaar paused then leaned forward, their expression darkening. "*I*, however, believe you to be a liability. A uniquely gifted soldier who actively *declined* all honours and advancements? At best, you have clearly never had any inclination towards self-improvement, which disgusts me. At worst you are a coward. Or perhaps even a traitor, unwilling to extend yourself for the benefit of the Dominion."

Sneet kept their cranium bowed, but their mandibles flexed in barely repressed anger.

All I ever wanted was to be a farmer, working the land and livestock alongside my family. But the war machine of Central rolls over everything, chewing up citizens and spitting out soldiers, any notable aptitudes repurposed as weapons. My skills could have been directed into a role in the public sector, or the diplomatic corps, or the medical industry—

—the clash of blade against blade, claws unsheathed and ready to disembowel—

No! Sneet desperately focussed upon thoughts of their farm, stifling the urge to attack.

"However," Kevlaar continued sharply, "despite *vigorous* objections on my part, Central *insists* that you be among the ten thousand operatives selected for this mission, so my claws are tied."

Sneet made a gesture of respectful acknowledgement. "I am honoured, Fleetlord. And…when is the mission scheduled to begin?"

"Appendix eight."

Sneet scrolled. *Frek!* Immediate *deployment??*

"Yet another inconvenience," Kevlaar grumbled resignedly. "There is an entire season of each local solar cycle devoted to the worship of the aforementioned sub-deity. Regretfully, the current season was well underway before Central noted the strategic importance of the planet, so any delay will result in the mission being pushed back significantly, and this, of course, is completely unacceptable. However, to compensate for the lack of prep time, a cultural lexicon comprising all available intel on this civilisation—behaviours, customs, social miscellany—will be downloaded directly to your frontal cortex. Between that, the support of your implant, and your own noted abilities, Central believes you will be fully equipped to succeed." They fixed Sneet with another cold stare. "So. Be sure to succeed."

The words promised dire consequences for failure.

Sneet bowed again. "As you command, Fleetlord. Earth shall belong to the G'norr Dominion."

The phantom smell of burning bodies tickled their olfactory cilia, then vanished.

"Yes," Sneet said carefully. "I was sent by the agency." In the event that Jeremy decided to check this claim, g'norr A.I.s were standing by to provide confirmation across a variety of indigenous communication platforms.

"Huh. I didn't realise we'd managed to book anyone else, but that's excellent! As far as I'm concerned Stan can go whistle, the worthless—" Jeremy shook his head. "Anyway, mustn't dawdle. Come along, you're on!" He grasped Sneet's sleeve. "And lose the bottle."

Sneet put the bottle down atop the cistern and—after super-magnetising the lock on the cubicle door to ensure Stan's cocoon wouldn't be interfered with—allowed themself to be led from the bathroom and down a series of corridors, finally arriving at a large set of double doors.

"Wait here." Jeremy opened the door a crack and slipped through. A wall of noise blasted through the gap, pummelling Sneet's aural membranes. It sounded like—

—*queskin berserkers screeching as they cascade over the top of the trench, sonic cleavers slicing through g'norr troops like c-beams through mist—*

Sneet's claws jerked instinctively towards the atomiser tucked into their belt.

`stand down—wait and assess situation`

Focus! Think of the farm!

I miss my farm…

"Well hello, children!" Sneet heard Jeremy call out above the noise. "May I have your attention please?"

There was a susurrus of exaggerated shushing that did exactly nothing to reduce the pandemonium.

"I know you've all been waiting a while, for which Frankston Mall apologises, and we're very grateful for your patience, and I'm very happy to announce that our *very special visitor* from the North Pole has finally arrived! Can everybody tell me who it is?"

"SANTA CLAUS!" screamed the unseen crowd (although Sneet could have sworn they heard a lone voice shout "BLUEY!"). The door flew open. Light blazed in Sneet's optics as they were grabbed by the arm and dragged forth. They blinked, finding themselves standing on the perimeter of a large indoor quadrangle. Before them, a low white picket fence decorated with red-and-white striped poles and clumps of white fibrous-looking material encircled a large, raised dais. A small gate in the fence near to where Sneet stood opened onto a short path which led up to the dais, upon which stood a heavily decorated, high-backed throne. Suspended from the ceiling above the throne was a large painted sign that read 'Santa's Grotto.'

Sneet, who had seen multiple instances of bloody action in grottos, immediately decided that any race too stupid to know what actually constituted a grotto deserved to be conquered.

Beside the throne stood a garishly artificial plant, tall and conical and festooned with long loops of paper that hung from its branches. On the far side of the dais another path led to a second gate, and just beyond that stood a large mob of adult humans, their eyes fixed upon Sneet, a collective expression of (according to the download) aggressive resentment on their faces. And massed about the legs of the adults—

Frek! There are multitudes *of them!*

The crowd of human younglings resembled nothing less than a horde of ravenous grettlers; eyes wide and staring, mouths agape and bawling.

A wave of moist air, heavy with the stench of sweat and hormones and faeces swept across Sneet's cilia—

—drowning in the humidity of the Frelt jungle, firing desperately as their battalion goes down beneath the pincers and leech-tongues of the cthuti swarm—

Sneet quivered, claws inching towards the atomiser.

`delay defensive response—assess situation`

A sharp nudge in the thorax interrupted Sneet's panic attack. "Well? Off you go, then!"

With an effort, Sneet tore their optics from the horde and stared at Jeremy.

"For goodness' sake, give them a wave!" Jeremy hissed.

Relevant information trickled from Sneet's download. Sneet hesitantly raised a claw and undulated their digits. The younglings screeched maniacally.

"What's wrong?" Jeremy demanded. "Why are you being so…*stiff?* Are you *new* at this or something?"

"I am," Sneet admitted.

Jeremy groaned. "Oh for—look, just go and sit on the throne. You can work it all out from there, I hope…"

Sneet slowly walked up to the throne and took a seat, surreptitiously activating the tiny REU unit affixed to their wrist as their implant ran a quick procedural reminder:

`younglings sequentially mount santa and relate their demands—acquiesce to reduce resistance to algorithm`

`<Confirmed. Check output now>`

++the g'norr are your friends—welcome them—love, serve, obey—the g'norr are your friends++ output verified

"Nice of you to join us." Sneet started as a small human female suddenly appeared at their side, sneering at them as she pointlessly adjusted a tiny green skirt that barely covered her posterior. "Another liquid lunch?" She blinked. "Oh, sorry! Where's Stan? Who're you?"

"Stan has been relieved of employment. I am John."

"Oh. Well. Okay, John. Keep your hands off my arse and we'll get along just fine." The female bared her teeth at Sneet; a display that anywhere else in the galaxy would have heralded a violent death. Sneet fought the instinctive urge to recoil.

A smile, the download offered. *An expression of welcome and benevolence.*

"I'm Tina, by the way," the female added. "A.K.A. 'Mary Christmas.' Hilarious, huh? Anyway, glad you're here." She nodded towards the crowd, adjusting her skirt again. "This lot's about to riot. So—ready to go?"

"I truly am!" Sneet admitted.

Tina gave them a look.

"…ready to go," Sneet continued unconvincingly, as the download belatedly supplied context, "to the first subject. *Child!* Begin. Ready to *begin* with the first child, I mean."

Tina gave Sneet another longer look. "Riiiiight…"

Sneet cringed inwardly. *Frek! The sooner I get this over and done with, the better. Then I can get back to skutchharvest and—*

Blazing light, as from a low-yield nuclear device going off, seared Sneet's optics.

"*ARGH!*" Sneet rocked backwards, almost toppling the throne.

—*the sickly-sweet stench of melted tallow, bodies burst open by the pressure of the blast*—

"Oi! Trevor! A little warning next time?" Tina called out irritably.

Sneet painfully blinked away the flash-blindness and saw a corpulent human male standing a few metres in front of the so-called grotto, fussing over a device that looked suspiciously like an antimatter generator with a large tripod-mounted reflective light projector (*laser cannon?*) standing alongside. Both devices were pointed directly at Sneet, who shrank back into the throne.

primitive media-recording apparatus designed to produce still images of the target

Sneet exhaled slowly, claws still tightly gripping the arms of the throne. *<Why was that information not included in the download??>*

omissions are inevitable—a note has been uploaded to central

The human male glanced up from his equipment. "Yeah, my fault, sorry! I thought Santa already had a kid on his knee!" He waved at Sneet. "Hi, Santa!"

Sneet grudgingly waved back.

"Why aren't you wearing your glasses?" Tina demanded of Trevor.

"Don't need 'em anymore," Trevor called out proudly, clearly addressing the artificial tree to Sneet's right. "Had Lasik surgery!"

"When?"

"This morning!" Trevor beamed.

"Riiiiight…"

"Anyhoo, sorry again. I'll give you a heads-up next time."

"Appreciated!" Tina turned to Sneet. "Ready?"

Sneet shot another look at the waiting mob and nodded tightly. Taking Sneet's response to Tina as a signal, an aging security guard standing nearby shuffled closer. "Why does that guard look so apprehensive?" Sneet asked.

Tina glanced at the guard. "Does he?"

"I can smell his anxiety from here."

Tina shrugged, "Well, I s'pose he's just staying alert. You know, just in case."

"In case of what, exactly?" Sneet demanded, but Tina had already moved away, smiling brightly as she pushed open the entry gate.

"Okay, children!" Tina called, above the din. "Everybody in line? One at a time, please. Who's first?" She reached out, grasped the hand of the nearest youngling, and led him up onto the dais before bending to quietly confer with him. The youngling muttered something. Tina nodded. "Santa, this is Troy."

respond

"Greetings, Troy." Sneet favoured the youngling with a tight smile. The youngling bared his teeth in response. Sneet shuddered.

Silence.

"Troy, aren't you going to say hello to Santa?" Tina asked encouragingly.

"'lo Sanna," the youngling mumbled.

"Come on, up onto Santa's knee!" Assisted by Tina, the youngling scaled Sneet's leg—delivering several optic-watering kicks to Sneet's cloaca—and perched precariously upon their patella.

Teeth gritted against the pain, Sneet waited for the youngling to present his demands.

More silence.

prompt required

"So, Troy," Sneet said, "what do you wish me to bring you for Christmas?"

++the g'norr are your friends—welcome them—accept their rule—love, serve, obey++

The youngling chewed his lip thoughtfully, gazing up at Sneet. "Truck?"

A quick sift provided context. "A truck." Sneet nodded. "I believe this could possibly be something I might perhaps supply to you."

linking you to the REU—deliver reinforcement

Sneet glanced at Tina to ensure she wasn't observing them too scrupulously, then leaned in closer to the youngling, staring into his eyes. *<Who do you serve?>* they projected.

The youngling stared mutely at Sneet.

++the g'norr are your friends—welcome them—love, serve, obey++

<Well?> Sneet pressed.

The youngling's eyes glazed over for a moment, indicating the algorithm had successfully tapped into whatever passed in humans for a frontal cortex. Then he frowned, hands fidgeting. "The…gnaw?"

`<Excellent>`

`embed subliminal directive`

`<Now forget all I have said until otherwise`
`directed>`

The youngling nodded.

"Very well," Sneet said loudly. "Go! Await your gifts!"

FLASH!

"*ARGH!*"

—blinding glare as burning chemicals spray across foliage and soldiers alike, scorching Sneet's optics before their goggles can dim. They scream in agony—

"Sorry!" Trevor called out. "I thought the kid was about to make a run for it!"

Sneet blinked myopically as Tina stepped forward and assisted the youngling in dismounting Sneet's leg. "There you go, Troy. Say goodbye to Santa!"

"Bye, Sanna."

Tina led the youngling to the exit, where two adult humans took possession, smiling and pressing their spawn for information as they walked off towards the photo collection point. Sneet sat back, feeling quite pleased with themself despite their still-smarting optics. They had forgotten the buzz of exercising power over lesser beings; the intoxicating sense of superiority—

—the guttural burp of plasma cannons, enemy troops boiled into fine mist—

Sneet exhaled tightly, refocussing. *This will not be difficult. I shall be back on my farm in no time.*

The next three younglings also proved relatively easy to process (Sneet even remembering to direct their optics downwards to avoid the debilitating flash of the camera), although repeatedly having to reinforce the algorithm quickly became tedious. But Sneet had endured worse in the field, and promises of a toy aeroplane, a 'Barbie' and a

'Nintendo Switch' tripped effortlessly off their tongue while the younglings sat and nodded, eyes glazed as the algorithm sowed the seeds of submission in their minds, before being sent running happily back to their progenitors—

Parents, the download offered. *'Father' for male parent, 'Mother' for female.*

And then—

"You're not the *real* Santa!"

Sneet jerked in panic, almost tipping the sneering youngling off their leg as they grabbed for their atomiser. *Discovered!*

delay defensive response—await confirmation of hostile intent

"Of *course* he's the real Santa, Charles." Tina laid a supportive hand on Sneet's shoulder. "Isn't that right, Santa?"

Sneet nodded, pulmonary glands pulsing furiously. "Yes. I am the real Santa." They forced a smile. "Why would you think otherwise?"

The youngling probed his nasal orifice with a practised finger. "My brother says you're not the real Santa, 'cos if you're the real Santa then how come they got a Santa over at Southlands who says *he's* the real Santa, and the Langwarrin mall too, and you can't *all* be the real Santa, so he says you're all lying and *none* of you is the real Santa." Charles paused, examining a lump of something unthinkable wedged under his fingernail. "You're a *faker!*"

Against all logic, Sneet felt personally affronted by the accusation. "I am not a faker," they said, stiffly. "I am the genuine Santa."

"Are not."

"I am."

"Not!"

"Am!"

"*NOT!*"

"*AM!!!*"

Charles favoured Sneet with an expression of contempt worthy of a g'norr drill instructor. "*Prove* it!"

Sneet considered. "Very well. Tell me, how is it that I am able to visit all homes upon this world on a single night of the year?"

A careless shrug. "Magic."

"That…is correct. So, if I employ *magic*," Sneet continued, unable to keep the tone of utter derision from their voice, "then why would I not also use magic to appear simultaneously at every commercial outlet on Earth?" A pause. "Well?"

++the g'norr are your friends—welcome them++

The youngling's eyes glazed, regarding Sneet blankly for a moment. Then:

"Shove it up your arse!" he squealed, and was off and running for the exit before Sneet's download could finish providing a translation.

FLASH!

"*ARGH!*"

—arcs of incandescent superheated plasma melting through the sides of descending troop carriers—

"Sorry!"

"Kid's already gone, Trevor," Tina called out.

"Really?" Trevor straightened up and blinked. "I could have sworn… Huh. Well, maybe Santa needs to lose a bit of the old midsection, eh?" He chuckled, slapping a hand against his own arguably excessive belly. "I could have sworn all that extra padding was a kid!"

"Moron," Tina muttered to Sneet. "And how about the mouth on that kid! If *I'd* talked to adults that way when I was that age…"

"Immediate ritual disembowelment!" Sneet finished, nodding in agreement.

"What??"

"I…said nothing."

subject escaped processing—unacceptable!

<Apologies, but—>

unacceptable!

Sneet scowled at the cacophonous mass of primates nearby. *<I wish to raise a concern with Central>*

proceed

<Even with the reduced capacity of these REUs, the algorithm should be fully accessing the

human cortex, with my reinforcement simply giving an extra 'push.' However, that last youngling seemed to ignore the algorithm altogether>

A pause.

observation supported

<Well, I understand this supposition contradicts accepted wisdom regarding Level Three civilisations, but...could sensory overstimulation due to the crowded location be interfering with processing? I mean, is it possible that a Level Three species could be so easily distracted?>

A longer pause.

observation provisionally supported—a note has been uploaded to central

Frek! Sneet thought. *How did these humans achieve a Level Three civilisation with such impaired cognitive wiring? This is what comes from Central rushing into this mission without full intel...*

"For what it's worth," Tina said, noting Sneet's dark expression, "I thought you handled that pretty well."

Sneet nodded curtly. "I...appreciate your evaluation. Thank you," they added, after a quick sift.

Tina smiled, before moving to acquire the next youngling. "This is Nigel, Santa."

"Greetings, Nigel. And what do you wish me to bring you for Christmas?"

++the g'norr are your friends—welcome them—love, serve, obey++

Without making optical contact with Sneet, the youngling pulled a folded-up piece of paper from the breast pocket of his immaculately pressed button-up shirt. "I," he said, with an air of self-importance that Sneet thought surpassed that of most System Overlords, "have a list."

Sneet smiled tightly. "Indeed?"

"I want," Nigel continued, unfolding the paper into something resembling a full-sized stellar map, "a PlayStation Five, a red Prevelo bicycle, a Spider-Man Aqua-Attack figure, a premium badminton set, a boxed set of Derwent artists' coloured pencils, a Racin' Rager Speedboat, a pair of Nike Air Max Plus Light Photography Printed Mesh sneakers, a trampoline, a Totem-Tennis set, a SpyraThree Water Blaster, an iPhone Sixteen, the new Fortnite game for PlayStation Five, a Fortnite logo 3D bedside lamp, a Fortnite pencil case—"

"*Enough!*" Sneet snapped. The youngling looked up, a look of annoyance wrinkling his chubby features. To Sneet's dismay, Nigel's eyes seemed bright and unbothered by the algorithm.

`<The Id is strong with this one. Flag with`
`Central as an addendum to previous note>`

`flagged`

`++the g'norr are your friends—welcome them—`
`love, serve, obey++`

`<Let me tell you what I shall bring,>` Sneet projected, leaning in towards the youngling. `<I shall bring the g'norr, your new masters. Do you understand?>`

The youngling glanced down at his list, then back at Sneet.

`<Well? Who do you serve?>`

Nigel shrugged

`<It is the g'norr, yes?>` Sneet urged.

Nigel frowned. "I suppose."

Sneet nodded triumphantly.

"Smile for the camera!" Trevor miraculously remembered to call out. Sneet averted their optics. There was a slight pause. "There's still a kid there, right?"

"Yes!" Tina confirmed tersely.

FLASH!

`<Now forget, until otherwise directed>` Sneet ordered. "You may go!" they added out loud, pointing towards the exit.

Nigel dismounted and trudged away, glancing back at Sneet with an unreadable expression on his face.

do not deviate from mission specifications—
acquiescing to youngling demands supports the
algorithm
<But—>
do not deviate

Sneet huffed in annoyance, turning to regard their next subject.

"This is Vanessa, Santa."

"Greetings, Vanessa. What do you wish me to bring you for Christmas?"

++the g'norr are your friends—welcome them—
love, serve, obey++

The youngling mumbled something.

"I cannot hear you," Sneet said impatiently. "You are speaking too quietly to be heard by the human ear, which is of course what I am equipped with. Please speak more loudly and clearly."

"Wan' Daddy."

<What?>
await clarification

"I see," Sneet said cautiously. "Kindly provide further explanation."

Vanessa's lip quivered. "Mummy says Daddy's in Heaven, an' I really miss him, an' Mummy still cries at night 'cos she misses him too, an' if you bring Daddy back for Christmas I don' mind if you give my presents to some'n' else." To Sneet's alarm, tears began to well up in the corner of the youngling's eyes. "*Please?*"

<Context?>
hypothesis: the male parent of the youngling
is deceased—she is requesting the parent be
revived
<Oh, for—even this stupid primate must
realise that—>
acquiesce

Freksake! "Vanessa," Sneet began sternly.

The youngling stared miserably, looking not unlike a skutchling newly separated from its brood queen, and Sneet felt a sudden twinge.

They hesitated, then took a deep breath. "Vanessa. I regret to advise that I will be unable to—"

do not deviate!—acquiesce!

"That is, I do not believe it is physically possible for me to—"

The youngling began to sob, tears pouring down her reddening cheeks.

—the weeping of shattered soldiers, bleeding out into the dirt—

expressing grief

<Yes! I worked that out for myself!>

Hence my being assigned to this ridiculous mission, Sneet thought to themself sourly. "Hush!" they hissed.

Vanessa ceased crying, her breath hitching brokenly.

Sneet performed a hasty sift. *<I cannot access any relevant advisory information! Please assist!>*

searching...

A pause.

<Well??>

central trusts in your experience and abilities

Sneet opened their mouth, then closed it again, then thought some very bad words, then took a moment to collect their thoughts. "Vanessa. Listen to me."

++the g'norr are your friends—welcome them++

The youngling's eyes misted over slightly.

"Death comes to all biological life," Sneet went on, in what they hoped was a kind but matter-of-fact tone, "and no known power in the universe can permanently reverse the process, even with expert medical application of invasive organobionics, or parasites that can override neurological function. Therefore it is best for you to simply spend a moment of silence in memory of the fallen, then forget them as best you can and rejoin the battle—er, that is, continue on with your life. Without dying. Until you inevitably *do* die, of course." They paused. "I hope this advice assists you in dealing with your loss."

Behind them, Sneet heard Tina hiss "What the actual *fuck*, dude??"

The youngling continued to stare up at Sneet for moment. Then she began to wail loudly.

FLASH!

"ARGH!"

"Sorry! I thought she was smiling for the camera!"

Sneet squinted angrily through the dark spots strobing their vision. Several of the waiting adult humans were regarding them suspiciously. One particular female, undoubtedly Vanessa's mother, glared at them from the sidelines.

"Oh, very well!" Sneet growled irritably. "I shall bring you your daddy for Christmas!"

The crying ceased instantly. Vanessa beamed at Sneet.

<And your new masters, the g'norr!> Sneet projected, without enthusiasm. *<To love, serve and obey...etcetera!>*

She nodded excitedly.

<Now forget, until otherwise directed> "Go now." Sneet's leg was quickly vacated, then re-occupied. "Greetings—" they began, then let out a bellow of disgust as hot, evil-smelling liquid began to soak through the left leg of their trousers. *"Trask devour you, filthy demonspawn!"* The youngling fled, squealing.

FLASH!

"*WHY??*" Sneet roared, visions of imploding battledroids flickering before their traumatised optics.

"Sorry! I thought he was still on your knee!"

Tina tapped Sneet on the shoulder. "You should probably go and clean up."

"*Really?* Had you not suggested it, I may well have sat here in blissful ignorance for the remainder of the day, marinating in urine!"

"Ah, shove it up your arse, John. I'm just trying to help. You know where the bathroom is." She jerked a thumb towards the door from which Sneet had entered the quadrangle. "Go clean up, and I'll stall the mob."

Inwardly cursing, Sneet rose and stalked towards the door, the sensation of sodden fabric slapping against their leg reminding them of the horrors of jungle-borne wet-rot. Behind them, they could hear Tina doing her best to cover their departure. "Santa just has to go and check on his reindeer—" wails of protest from younglings and adults alike, "—but he'll be back very soon, so if I could just ask you to be a little bit patient…"

At this moment I would ecstatically trade having to deal with these human younglings for the horrors of unarmed combat against a nest of raging swarfs. Swarfs do not demand gifts. Swarfs do not tell you to shove anything up your arse. They certainly do not urinate upon you, unless involuntarily during torture. They just die when you shoot them. Frek, even skutchlings *have more self-control than these youngling primates!*

My poor, sweet skutchlings—

Utterly preoccupied, Sneet almost collided with Jeremy, who was looking extremely harried. Sneet briefly wondered if that was Jeremy's default expression. "I was just coming to get you." Jeremy glanced down. "Oh dear. Did a child pee on you?"

"Your powers of observation astound me."

"Right. Well, occupational hazard, I suppose. Anyway," Jeremy continued, ignoring Sneet's glare, "I've had a complaint from one of the parents, and I just need you to come and help smooth the water a bit. It shouldn't take a moment. Then you can go and clean up." He offered what Sneet's download suggested was a wholly insincere smile.

Sneet narrowed their optics suspiciously. "Would it not be more sanitary, and less unpleasant for all, for me to wash the urine out of my clothes *before* meeting with the complainant?"

Jeremy licked his lips. "The complainant is being rather…insistent."

Sneet glanced longingly towards the door leading to the bathroom. "Very well. But let us make this quick. My skin is beginning to burn." How the acidic liquid had managed to seep all the way through a thick layer of fabric *and* several layers of human-looking syntheskin was utterly beyond Sneet, but it was an issue they very much intended to raise with Central.

Jeremy nodded and motioned Sneet to follow him, heading off towards a small alcove further away from the door to the bathroom than Sneet would have liked. As they got closer, and Sneet saw who was occupying the alcove, their pulmonary glands sank. It was the youngling named Nigel, accompanied by two human adults, presumably his parents.

"What sorta crap you been tellin' my kid?" demanded Nigel's father, a large, hirsute specimen with a conversely hairless cranium, wearing a paint-spattered flannelette shirt.

"Sir, please!" Jeremy raised a placating hand. "I'm sure this is just a simple misunderstanding. Let's give Santa a chance to explain, shall we?"

Nigel's father's face turned a shade of purple that Sneet's download identified as atypical in humans. "You callin' my son a *liar?!*" Several bystanders turned to stare. "You callin' him a goddamn *liar?!*"

"Nicholas darling, please don't make a scene," chided Nigel's mother, an elegant woman as immaculately dressed as her son.

Nigel's father ignored her, pushing a bloated finger so deeply into the front of Sneet's suit that it pressed painfully against their thoracic plate. Sneet fought the urge to remove the offending finger from the offender's hand. "My kid says Santa refused to bring him any toys!"

"I'm sure that's not…" Jeremy turned to Sneet, eyebrows raised. "Santa?"

"I did not refuse," Sneet said, truthfully.

"I started reading my list," Nigel whined, "and he wouldn't listen!"

Nigel's father glowered at Sneet. "Well?"

Jeremy favoured Nigel with a patronising smile, "Look, I'm sure we all understand that Santa doesn't like to actually *promise* to bring what you ask for, because sometimes he runs out of particular toys, so promising could put *Santa*—" and here he glanced pointedly at Nigel's father, "—in an awkward position. But that's not the same thing as *refusing* to bring toys, is it?"

Nigel's mother looked up at her husband, rubbing his arm gently. "There you are, darling. It was all just a silly miscommunication, that's all."

Nigel's father seemed to relax slightly, his facial hue shifting from almost black to merely aubergine.

Jeremy turned back to Nigel. "So that's why Santa just says he'll *try* to bring what you asked for."

Ah, frek, Sneet thought.

Nigel's lip started to quiver. "He didn't say anything like that! All he said was that he was going to bring some new masters who I had to serve, and they were called the gnaw!"

Sneet stared at the youngling. *Impossible!*

"Gnaw?" Nigel's father growled at Sneet. "Masters? What kinda crap is this? You some kinda pervert?"

<Priority! Check REU for errors!>

checking—no errors—reinforce processing

Sneet quickly crouched down beside Nigel. *<Forget all that was told to you of the g'norr! Forget!>*

"I'm sure Santa wouldn't have said anything of the sort!" Jeremy protested.

"Goddamn it!" Nigel's father snarled. "Call my kid a liar again and I'll shove my fist so far up your arse—!"

What is this obsession humans have with arses?

<Do you understand, youngling? Forget until otherwise directed!>

"Nicholas, please, do remember your blood pressure!"

"You awful man!" Everyone turned to regard the distressed-looking human female striding towards them, dragging the youngling Vanessa alongside her. "How *could* you!"

"Please, madam!" Jeremy now seemed on the verge of panic. People were actually leaving the queue to Santa's Grotto to hurry over and investigate the escalating situation in the alcove. Sneet was reminded far too vividly of the experience of being pinned down in a trench by approaching enemy footsoldiers. Even the security guard began to drift across, hand hovering idly over his holster.

The newly arrived female glared at Jeremy whilst levelling an accusing finger at Sneet. "How *dare* your Santa tell Vanessa her father's coming home for Christmas? Her father's *dead!*"

There was a shocked intake of breath from the gathering crowd.

Then silence.

Then a single voice from the back of the crowd said: "Ohhh, shit!"

`prioritise reinforcement`

`<I know!>` "Do you understand?" Sneet hissed to Nigel. `<Forget!>`

"Forget what?" Nigel whined plaintively. "The gnaw, or the presents?"

`<The g'norr! Forget the g'norr!>`

"Excuse me?" Another human couple appeared beside Nigel's parents. "Sorry, we couldn't help overhearing. Troy—" the female of the couple nodded towards her own youngling, "—said exactly the same thing about Santa bringing the gnaw, or gnawing on him, or something. That was right, wasn't it, Troy?"

Troy nodded. "The gnaw. To love, serve and obey."

"We thought he was just mucking around. Y'know, like kids do. But then we heard what *you* were saying, and—"

`reinforce processing`

`<I KNOW!>` Sneet spun on their haunches, glaring at Troy. `<Forget! I command you to *forget!*>`

"*Excuse* me?" Troy's father snapped. "*What* did you just say to my son??"

Oh, so now *the processing works!* Sneet stood up and met the human's gaze unblinkingly. "I...said nothing."

"I certainly didn't hear him say anything, darling," Troy's mother interjected.

"That's because my hearing's better than yours now, Carol." Troy's father held a finger to one of his ears, indicating a small electronic device nestled there. "These new hearing aids pick up *everything!*"

"I...didn't even see his lips move, Simon..."

Troy's father frowned. "Well…you know these Santas often have other acting jobs. This one can probably do ventriloquism…"

<Ventriloquism?>

The download offered an explanation.

<I…am I even awake right now??>

"She's been in therapy for *months!*" Vanessa's mother wailed. "She misses her father *so much!* Do you have any idea how much damage you've done? *Do you?!*"

"Look, please, madam," Jeremy said desperately, "I'm sure this is all just a huge misunderstanding!"

maintain control of situation
<How? Advise!>
assessing…assessing…please wait…

"I'm so very sorry for your loss." Nigel's mother laid a comforting hand on Vanessa's mother's arm. "It must be so difficult for you both. And at Christmas, too."

"Well, thank you." Vanessa's mother managed a tight smile, then shot a glance at her daughter to check if she was listening before leaning closer to Nigel's mother and whispering, at a volume Sneet felt could have raised the fallen, "Look, he's not actually dead—that's just what I told *her.* To protect her, y'know? Bastard ran away with the TV repairman. I *wish* he was dead!"

assessing…please wait…

Sneet furiously straightened their back, allowing their interlocked sternal rings to separate and expand. The surrounding crowd backed away slightly at the sight of Santa suddenly appearing to grow a full half-metre taller, visibly straining the stitching of his crimson suit. "ALL OF YOU!" Sneet shouted angrily, sweeping the crowd with a glare. "Give me your attention!" *<Priority! Maximise output and range of REU!>*

++THE G'NORR ARE YOUR FRIENDS—WELCOME THEM—LOVE, SERVE, OBEY++

The eyes of the crowd, younglings and adults alike, became vacant and unfocussed. There was a moment of silence.

Then…

One of the younglings standing nearby—*Charles*, Sneet recalled bitterly—blinked slowly, smirked, pointed at Vanessa and snorted with spiteful glee. "Your mummy says your daddy ran *awaa-aay!*" he sang.

Vanessa immediately burst into tears.

"Oh, you little shit!" Vanessa's mother spat.

'Hoy!" snapped another woman, presumably Charles' mother. "Don't you dare speak to my son like that!"

"*Be silent!*" Sneet snarled. "All of you! Look at me and hear my words!"

++THE G'NORR ARE YOUR FRIENDS—WELCOME THEM—LOVE, SERVE, OBEY++

<OBEY AND FORGET!>

"Your daddy ran *awaa-aay!* Your daddy ran *awaa-aay!*" Charles repeated mockingly. "*My* mummy an' daddy an' me all live in our house *together*, an' th' smorning I went in their room an' Daddy was jumping up an' down on Mummy's tummy while he was lying on top of her an' Mummy was crying really loud an' I smacked Daddy on the bum an' yelled BAD DADDY!—*WAAAAAAAAH!*" he added, as his crimson-faced mother yoinked him by the neck of his shirt and dashed away.

reinforce processing—still assessing situational requirements...

"Vanessa, sweetie, darling!" Vanessa's mother crouched down protectively by her child. "Are you okay, sweetie?"

Vanessa choked on her sobs, took a deep breath and let out a nerve-shredding scream—

—a terrifying screech shreds the silence of the savannah. Fighting the urge to flee, Sneet assumes the warrior's pose, a range of bladed weapons gripped in their tentacles, one claw holding a ten-shot pulse bazooka, the other lightly pressed to the tab of the suicide grenade slung from their harness as the swarm of klettan arachnoids gallops towards them—

"This is all your fault!" Vanessa's mother barked at Jeremy, whose face had now assumed the colour and consistency of gelatine. "I'm going to *sue* this mall, and you and your Santa personally, for *every cent you own!* Do you have any idea how much therapy *costs? Do you??"*

"Madam, *please!"* Jeremy begged weakly.

"What sorta setup you runnin' here, you sonofabitch!" Nigel's father demanded, thrusting his chest into Jeremy's personal space.

"Sir, please, if you'd just give me a moment to—"

"Sir?" The security guard moved closer, eyeing Nigel's father warily as he unclipped his holster. "Could you please take a couple of steps back?"

"You called security on me??" Nigel's father squealed.

"What?? No!! I've been here with you for the last five minutes!! When could I possibly have—??" Jeremy directed a pacifying gesture towards the guard. "It's okay, Roger, I've got this under control."

`reinforce processing`

Sneet gritted their teeth. *This cannot be happening! How can these accursed primates possibly resist reprogramming when the algorithm is so clearly being received and understood? Unless…*

No. Impossible.

Sneet bent down over Nigel. "Tell me," they hissed urgently, "what do you wish me to bring you for Christmas?"

Nigel took an involuntary step backwards, then puffed out his chest defiantly. "I *told* you! I want a PlayStation Five, a red Prevelo bicycle, a Spider-Man Aqua-Attack figure—"

`<NO! Listen and obey!>` Sneet stared deeply into Nigel's eyes. `<I shall bring new masters, the g'norr! That is what you want for Christmas!>`

`++THE G'NORR ARE YOUR FRIENDS—WELCOME THEM— LOVE, SERVE, OBEY++`

Nigel's expression went blank for a moment. Then he shook his head. "I want a *PlayStation Five!"*

An icy claw seemed to close around Sneet's pulmonary glands. They slowly stood up again and swept the crowd with a look of utter dismay. `<Frek! The one time Central fails to perform due diligence in gathering intel on a`

newly discovered civilisation…! These humans do not *operate like other previously-encountered sentient species, ruled by Id with a trace of Ego! Against all logic, they exist* simultaneously in both *states—sentient* and *animal! Sufficiently intelligent for the algorithm to tap into their central cortex, yet synchronously influenced by such levels of personal craving that—when reprogramming commences—their animalistic fixations immediately engage and negate the effects of re-education! Which means—>*

Sneet quivered.

<—which means there is no way this mission can succeed!>

supposition supported—a note has been up-loaded to central—await feedback—proceed with reinforcement

<IT IS NOT WORKING!>

additional verbal endorsement suggested

With a growing sense of dread, Sneet bent down to face Nigel again. "Nigel! *Listen and focus!*" *<You! Will! Accept! The g'norr!>*

"*Daddeee!!* He's talking about the gnaw again!"

"*Sonofabitch!*" Nigel's father delivered a sharp shove to Jeremy's shoulder. "You better get your Santa in line right now, or I'm gonna—!"

"Sir!" The security guard now had his weapon drawn, a snub-nosed plastic firearm pointed unsteadily at the floor. "Move back *right now!* I won't tell you again!"

"*I want a PlayStation Five! Give me a PlayStation Five, you stupid man!*"

Sneet reared up, glaring at the youngling. *I could crush you like a mollusc! Disembowel you with my spurs! Tear you apart! Atomise you!*

alert!—intentions exceed allowable behaviour!—stand down!—stand down!

<But—!>

a report has been uploaded to central!—disciplinary action will be advised!

And just like that, Sneet's fury evaporated.

<I...comply>

Coward! whispered a tiny voice in their hindbrain.

I know, Sneet thought miserably. *I am a coward. I do not stand up for myself. That is why I acquiesced to this ridiculous mission. That is why I cannot even assert my dominance over a human youngling. Because nobody respects me.*

Not even myself.

"PlayStation!!"

"Sonofabitch!"

"Sir!!"

"You awful man!!"

Something deep in Sneet's cerebral lobe snapped.

"*One more word, demonspawn,*" they snarled, glaring at Nigel, "*and I shall tear you open and spatter your guts across that artificial vegetation!*" Without breaking optical contact, Sneet pointed a claw towards the plastic tree beside Santa's throne.

There was a shocked silence. Then:

"*DADDEEEEE!!*"

"*SONOFABITCH!!*" Nigel's father screamed, charging towards Sneet. "*I'M GONNA KILL YOU!!*"

Sneet spun around to face the oncoming human. "I accept your challenge! In fact, I offer you the first strike, you foul, hairy, under-evolved *primate*!"

"I mean, the number of times *I've* wanted to tell a customer what I really thought of them…" Tina said, holding the icepack firmly to

Sneet's optical socket. "But to actually *do* it? Shit, man, I don't know whether that makes you a hero or a complete nutter, but mad props either way."

Sneet gave a non-committal grunt.

"And it was pretty cool seeing Nigel's dad get shot," Tina continued. "I'm assuming you missed that, given you were slightly comatose at the time."

"Was his death drawn out and agonising?" Sneet asked hopefully.

"Um...no. Roger tazed him, he did a little dance, then shat himself and fell over." Tina pulled the icepack away and frowned. "Huh. You're not even bruised. Given how hard he belted you, I thought—"

"I shall be fine, thank you," Sneet snapped, twisting on the toilet seat so they could turn their face away. The syntheskin had certain limits of realism. Underneath, their own flesh was no doubt turning an interesting shade of orange.

"Well, okay, if you're sure." Tina glanced at Jeremy, who was slumped against the cubicle door. From outside the bathroom, echoing up the corridor, came a steady collective roar of discontent. "Guess I'd better get out there and try to calm the animals. Again. I really don't get paid enough for this, Jeremy. And we clearly need a first aid station closer to Santa's Grotto."

"Yes! Thank you!" Jeremy stood back to let Tina past as she left the cubicle. "I'll bring it up with senior management!"

"Bullshit, Jeremy. Bullshit."

"What on *earth* were you *thinking?*" Jeremy demanded as Tina left. "You...you just can't *talk* to customers like that! I *know* the children are a mob of self-entitled little so-and-sos! I *know* the parents are even worse! But good golly! Threatening a *kid?* In front of his *parents?* And then challenging the parent to a *fight?*" He shook his head in utter disbelief. "What on *earth* is *wrong* with you?"

Sneet huffed wearily.

Jeremy rubbed his eyes, then gave an exasperated shrug. "Well. I've done some damage control. Gave the parents some vouchers. But...I mean, if it hadn't been for the fact that you were the one who was assaulted, the police probably would have arrested you for causing an affray! Frankly, I should absolutely fire you, except—" he stopped abruptly.

"Except that you have no other Santas to call upon," Sneet said quietly.

Jeremy made a nervously dismissive gesture. "That's neither here nor there. We're wasting time, so let's get you back out there, pronto!"

Sneet looked up sharply. "I beg your pardon?"

Jeremy gestured towards the bathroom door. "Get back out there! That crowd's going to tear the mall apart if Santa doesn't hop to it!"

Sneet opened their mouth to protest.

priority!—incoming from central: abort mission!—all operatives recalled!—abort mission!

<A complete recall? Immediate? Confirm!>

confirmed—action as soon as possible without alerting humans

Something major must have occurred, Sneet realised; something far exceeding their own abject failure. They stood up gingerly and favoured Jeremy with a smile that was just slightly too wide to be comfortably accommodated by their human disguise. Jeremy blanched and took a step back. "Jeremy," Sneet said, "I regret to inform you that I shall not 'hop to it.' Nor shall I any longer subject myself to the frankly—" they sifted for the appropriate local term, "—*inhumane* conditions of this workplace. I hereby resign my position as the Santa of Frankston Mall, and will be leaving the premises as soon as I have attended to my urine-soaked trousers."

Jeremy turned paler still. "No, hang on, wait a moment, just…look, we can discuss this after—"

"We cannot." Sneet pointed to the door. "Kindly leave."

Jeremy gawped for a moment, then pulled an expression that (according to Sneet's download) might have indicated either determination or constipation, and folded his arms across his chest. "Unacceptable. You are not leaving this mall until the end of your contracted shift at seven pm tonight. And I am not leaving your side until that time comes. Understand?"

Sneet briefly considered using the atomiser. But no; their own disappearance would cause enough suspicion without the additional mystery of a missing mid-level department store employee.

`priority: abort mission as soon as possible without alerting humans`

Which meant—

Sneet quivered. "But…there are at least a hundred of them out there!"

"A hundred? Goodness, yes. There *are* at least a hundred. *Now…*"

Iceworms crawled down Sneet's notochord. "What do you mean, *'now'*?"

"Oh, gosh, you really *must* be new at this. Those kids out there are just the early birds, the ones whose parents camp on the doorstep until the mall opens. By the time we close tonight we'll have had at least a *thousand* kids come through!"

"*A thousand??*"

"Indeed. So you'd best pull yourself together. Santa's Grotto has only been open for—" Jeremy consulted the timekeeping device on his wrist, "—forty-five minutes. Which means you still have seven hours and forty-five minutes to go. Not including your thirty-minute lunch break."

"Seven—?" Sneet teetered, steadying themself against the cubicle doorframe. "But—I do not *want* to!" they whined.

Jeremy's eye twitched slightly, and the corners of his mouth tweaked upwards into a smile that even Sneet could tell wasn't really a smile. "You know, I've just realised that I never actually asked you your name."

"John."

"Ah. Right. Well, John," the not-smile widened slightly, "I'll tell you what—you can take not wanting to do it, bundle it up nicely…and shove it up your arse." The eye twitched again. "How does that sound?"

Sneet stared at Jeremy.

Jeremy stared back.

"One moment, please," Sneet croaked, then staggered to the far cubicle, demagnetised the lock, and leaned across the cocoon to grab the half-empty bottle of scotch. *<Short-term effects upon g'norr physiology?>*

anticipating light physical anaesthesia, major decline in mental acuity—

<Excellent!> Sneet took a swig, choked, gasped, swigged again.

Jeremy appeared in the cubicle doorway. "My God! Are you *drinking?*"

Sneet carefully considered their answer. "Yes."

Jeremy clapped his hands to his head. "Oh my—! They don't *pay* me enough to put up with this! You can't go out there *drunk!*"

"So get someone else," Sneet growled, as an unfamiliar yet pleasant warmth bled from their gullet into their extremities. They took a final huge swig, then placed the now empty bottle atop the cistern with exaggerated precision, before sitting down on the toilet and attempting to wring as much urine from their trouser leg as possible. A thick yellow pool began to collect on the tiled floor at their feet.

"There *is* no-one else!" Jeremy spluttered.

Sneet glanced at him blearily. "Quite."

Jeremy glared at them. "You're just as bad as Stan!"

Sneet stood up and pushed past Jeremy, moving unsteadily towards the sink to wash the urine off their claws. "Stan," they slurred, "is obviously far more intelligent than either of us gave him credit for."

Sneet had never seen a superior officer so angry as Kevlaar looked right now.

The Fleetlord crouched silently in their web, glaring at their display. Sneet, who hadn't even been acknowledged yet, stood at the opposite end of the table, shifting uncomfortably.

After a very long silence, they coughed hesitantly.

Kevlaar looked up sharply and fixed Sneet with a look of absolute rage. "*A COMPLETE FAILURE!!*" they screamed. "*Every! Single!*

Operative! All encountering exactly the same range of issues as yourself! Failures, every last one of them!"

And how is that my *fault, you bloated malcontent?* The thought, angry and unthinkably insubordinate, flashed through Sneet's hindbrain before they could clamp down upon it. A small bleat of shock escaped their throat.

Kevlaar narrowed their optics. "You have something to say?"

Sneet bowed their cranium. *Will I ever see my farm again?* "No, Fleetlord. Apologies."

Coward!

Kevlaar regarded Sneet suspiciously for a moment, then turned their attention back to their display. "You may count yourself fortunate that Central lays all fault with their own intelligence and tech. However, despite this abysmal failure, they still assert the basic existing plan can be successful…once some adjustments have been made. Based upon the intel gleaned from Operation Santa, they have already begun to modify the algorithm and adjust the mission specs to target other widely held local ideologies. Going forward, operatives will deal with human younglings on a *completely* one-on-one basis, to eliminate all possible sources of distraction for those subjects." They pointed towards Sneet's display. "Observe the amended specifications."

Sneet stepped forward and regarded the scrolling text. "Operation Easter Bunny," they said tonelessly. "Operation Tooth Fairy."

"You will accept the mission?" It was barely a question; more a traditional invitation to comply.

Sneet stared blankly at Kevlaar. *So very like a human youngling. Petulant. Demanding. Disrespectful. When was the last time* you *saw combat, Fleetlord? Was it decades ago? Centuries? Have you, in fact,* ever *personally faced an enemy on the battlefield?* The screams of dying warriors echoed in their hindbrain. A tight smile tweaked the corners of their mouth, then slowly stretched into a full, toothy grin.

Kevlaar shrank back into their web at the sight.

Still grinning, Sneet slowly leaned forward and pressed their upper claws flat against the tabletop as they glared directly into Kevlaar's optics.

"With *all due respect*, Fleetlord," Sneet said, meaning every word of it, "you can take this mission…and shove it up your arse!"

Funny Peculiar
About the Stories

It's probably fair to say that I'm currently better known (as far as I'm known at all) for my short horror stories than for anything else*, and if you've purchased this collection thinking it was going to be filled with darkness and doom then I can only apologise. And no, I'm not returning your money. I have cats to feed.

It might surprise you, then, to know that science fiction—specifically humorous science fiction—was my sole focus when I first began publishing my work. I'd grown up watching what turned out to be a hugely influential combination of *The Goodies* and *Doctor Who* on television during the 1970s in Australia, and while my rather precocious reading interests as a child lay with more 'serious' authors such as Nicholas Fisk, H. G. Wells, and John Wyndham, by my pre-teen years I was diving into the works of Douglas Adams, Robert Sheckley, Eric Frank Russell, and other masters of comical SF.

---

* And for cat-related silliness, as per my 2023 book, *Conversations With My Cat*, which I suppose could also be considered a work of cosmic horror as it relates the trials of a lone man pitted against a dark and uncaring universe filled with entities utterly unconcerned with human existence. If you have cats, you'll know exactly what I mean.

Thus, from my first published work in 1999 through to around 2003 I almost exclusively wrote what I hoped readers would identify as humorous science fiction, and my complete output from that time forms the bulk of this collection wot you are reading right now, along with a small number of pieces published since. From 2003, however, I began to slide into considerably darker prose for a variety of reasons that I won't go into here, but which I can assure you were not fun. If you've a genuine interest in hearing about how deteriorating mental health can affect a writer (specifically me), there's a reasonably in-depth biography of sorts at the back of my collection of horror stories, *The Dark Man, By Referral and Less Pleasant Tales* (Daft Notions, 2024) that'll fill in the blanks for you. I've been informed by many that it's a pretty rough read, so don't say I didn't warn you. The handful of (intentionally) not-funny SF tales herein are mainly from that short transitional period between genres.

So there's your overview. Here's a few words about the individual stories.

Daily Grind

Quite a few of my stories, SF and horror alike, delve into various elements of working life, probably because so many aspects of employment strike me as weird, or hilarious, or horrific, or all three. Despite this, I've mostly enjoyed my working life over the past 35 years (generally as a retail manager), and have given every position I've ever held the best I was capable of at the time. As for those inevitable moments where everything that can go wrong does go wrong, or one encounters the employer or coworker or customer from hell...well, addressing such things in fiction is far cheaper than therapy. 'Daily Grind' was inspired by one particular coworker who constantly bemoaned the fact that they didn't even know why they bothered to do the deeply unsatisfying (to them) job they'd been doing for the past decade. They were extremely irritated by my suggestion that *money* was surely the greatest motivating factor, but I stand by that answer regardless because, despite being a creative person, I've always felt that very few people will ever truly be able to wholly support themselves by following their dreams, even if doing so feeds their creative soul. I'm not saying that I think people shouldn't have a crack at making a living from following their dreams, but I think it's also important to face the reality of requiring money to live, and will openly ridicule anyone who says things like 'I'd still work even if I didn't need the money.' That, sir, is utter crap. If most people didn't need the money they'd be doing exactly the same thing that I'd be doing under the same circumstances, which is retiring to a private island and spending my days watching horror movies from the comfort of my bed while eating cheese and onion chips. Anyone claiming otherwise is a dreadful fibber. Yeah, I said it.

Time Spent With a Cat

This story marked a return to writing after around fourteen years of being completely inactive (the reasons for which, again, are detailed in *The Dark Man, By Referral and Less Pleasant Tales*). I'd been sufficiently brash to announce on social media that I was working on a story for the first time in ages (hoping that mentioning it publicly would force me to actually finish it), and a few minutes later Lindy Cameron from Clan Destine Press sent me a DM, asking whether I'd be interested in submitting something to their forthcoming anthology of tales in which animals assist in solving crimes, *Who Sleuthed It?*. By sheer chance, the theme suited a vague story concept I'd had bumping around in my head since the early 1980s, after seeing a report on dissolvable metals on *Towards 2000*: a popular Australian show about current and possible future scientific developments. So: sometimes getting published is all down to just sitting on an idea for long enough, but mostly not, so don't please consider this as sound advice.

Ten Tales of Astounding Science Fiction

Many readers have, over the years, very courteously opined that I'm clearly a very cynical person in many ways, and that I seem to think the worst of society in general. I can't really fault this opinion, but—as inferred already—I do like to think that I manage to effectively funnel my cynicism and disappointment and rage at the state of the world into my writing, thus still managing to function in a socially acceptable way without resorting to arson.

Incident at Five Mile Creek

At the time I wrote this story I'd recently read A. Bertram Chandler's excellent alternate history novel, *Kelly Country*, and found myself wishing there were more alternate history tales about the notorious Australian bushranger. So, for better or worse, I wrote the story I wanted to read. I'd originally intended this as the first of several linked stories in which Kelly interacted with other events and characters—real and fictional—of the Victorian era: a sort of Australian *League of Extraordinary Gentlemen*, as it were. And as I get older, and more Victorian in my appearance, I find myself increasingly thinking I should pull my finger out and write those subsequent tales. Or have a brandy.

Marlowe Strawl

This was a bit of silliness I penned after thinking (very briefly) about the logical consequences of The Grandfather Paradox, so far as they relate to anyone ever getting to read about it after the fact.

Catflap

I've always loved tales of extraterrestrial beings, whether they're presented as being so inhuman that their machinations remain a mystery to the (human) reader or are written to embody certain recognisable traits of humanity for the purposes of commentary. Inimical aliens I find particularly compelling, although I'm a bigger fan of those that creep in through the back door—as occurs in John W. Campbell's *Who Goes There?* or Jack Finney's *The Body Snatchers*—than those who descend upon humanity *en masse* with all weapons blazing. 'Catflap' was my attempt to write a tale in which the aliens in question came across as funny *and* unsettling. Your mileage may vary, but I'm rather pleased with the result.

Full Circle

This story was inspired by my paternal grandmother's struggle with Parkinson's Disease, which very quickly robbed her of mental and physical health before her death, reducing her to an awful, vacant husk. The story punched me hard emotionally when I wrote it. When I dug it out again twenty years later to include in this collection, it punched even harder due to the recent death of my father from the same disease. It's hard to create flash fiction that carries any real emotional depth, given the restrictions on length, character development, and so on. But sometimes the subject matter alone carries you over the line, especially if it concerns a topic that affects so many people in the same way.

Alien Space Nazis Must Die!

I once again wore my cynicism on my sleeve with this story, which was born from my growing suspicion that most people would prefer to vanish into worlds of their own imagining—even at the cost of death— than deal with the unrelenting awfulness of reality. If your response to this is "Well, duh!," I'd like to point out that 'Alien Space Nazis Must Die!' was written and published in the earliest days of the Internet, and many years before the advent of modern Social Media. I'm not sure whether that makes this tale prescient or just a bit depressing, but the two seem so inextricably linked these days that it scarcely seems to matter. And yes, I know that I missed my true calling in writing motivational greetings cards.

Conquest!

Hey, did I ever tell you about the time I worked as an Amway representative for a year or so, and the insane levels of money-worshipping bullshit and gaslighting it exposed me to? No? Well, welcome to yet another of my stories written for the purposes of personal therapy.

Tools of the Trade

Another not-so-subtle dig at working culture; this time specifically addressing the dodgy shenanigans that so many employers engage in to secure staff fealty. As a long time employer myself I've always been a big fan of motivating staff by treating them like human beings with lives outside of work. Sadly, I seem to be increasingly in the minority with regards to this philosophy.

Catfish

This tale is original to this collection, written as a sort of companion to 'Conquest!' and similarly addressing one of the many possible shitty but mundane reasons that aliens might visit Earth. On a more personal note, I actually have no issues with online dating. Indeed, I greatly prefer it to many of the more old-fashioned ways of meeting a partner, especially as it relies so heavily upon honesty and in-depth discussions of values and opinions (ideally, at least, although—like everything else in life—it's certainly open to abuse). Anything that saves me from having to sit through five dates before finally discovering the person I'm wooing is a militant antivaxxer is okay in my book.

Andromeda Spaceways Pre-Booking Guide

When the Australian-based *Andromeda Spaceways Inflight Magazine*—a publication originally marketed as catering to the lighter side of speculative fiction—put out the call for submissions for their first issue, I saw an opportunity not just to be part of something that was generating a great deal of interest within the local spec-fic community, but to potentially showcase myself by securing the first piece that readers of the mag would see. I reached out to the editor with my pitch for a mock-booking guide for Andromeda Spaceways—an idea that perfectly fitted the central concept of the magazine—and they immediately took the bait, the fools! Despite this, the magazine has now been running successfully for over twenty-two years at the time of publishing this collection.

Old Habits Die

This was my very first published piece of flash fiction and, frankly, it shows. But in the interests of this being a complete collection of my SF work, here it is. It was inspired by my being told endlessly by more established writers (as well as by less established writers, writing manuals, complete strangers, and people who shout at bins) about the 'Show, Don't Tell' rule of writing. And it's absolutely a valid rule. But, being a bit of a shit-stirrer, I really wanted to see if I could write a half-decent story that kicked that rule out of the window. Half-decent may be overstating it.

Customer Service

Again with the sneaky aliens. But, as with my other sneaky alien stories, the aliens in question only ever see their plans succeed due to the general awfulness of humanity. I'm truly hoping life doesn't imitate art when aliens do in fact make themselves known to humanity, at least with regards to aliens being sneaky. Especially since life already depressingly imitates art with regards to humans being mostly awful.

Wiping the Smile Off

This piece was penned to prove, once and for all, that I am a twelve year old boy masquerading as a grown man.

Tragedy

Superheroes are a rich source of silliness, regardless of that particular well of satire having been largely drained over the past twenty-odd years, and I make no apologies for this piece, which of course basically amounts to a Dad Joke.

All I Want For Christmas

I like children. I have children of my own. And I think that most children have the capacity to be lovely, deeply inspiring creatures. Even those children who are demonstrably awful usually turn out to be so due to the behaviours and biases of the adults raising them. *However*…there is absolutely a tiny core of almost instinctive villainy and barbarism that resides deep in the psyche of even the most delightful child; a core that automatically engages the moment the child in question senses weakness in another, whether that other be a fellow child, an adult, an animal, or a carefully-arranged display of fragile crockery inherited from a beloved relative. This story was written to educate the ignorant masses of this inarguable truth, while also serving as personal therapy. It also includes both of my favoured tropes— sneaky aliens and awful workplace culture—and, being a Christmas story, works neatly as a convenient endpiece to this collection.

Acknowledgements

To the many authors whose work continues to inspire me to write.

To the editors who published my work, and the readers who told me they enjoyed it.

To the friends, family, and colleagues who supported me along the way.

To my parents, who told me to follow my dreams, and whom I miss every single day.

To Sarah, for absolutely everything.

Thank you.

About the Author

Chuck McKenzie was born in 1970 and is still not dead. He is an award-nominated author of numerous science fiction and horror stories, and he hopes one day to be described by his neighbours as having seemed like such a nice man. You can stalk him on the following platforms.

 @chuck.mckenzie.author

 @chuckmckenzieauthor

Also by Chuck McKenzie

Worlds Apart (Novel, Hybrid Publishers 1999)

AustrAlien Absurdities: Comic Tales of Science-Fiction, Fantasy & Horror by Australian Authors (Anthology, Co-edited with Tansy Rayner-Roberts, Agog! Press 2001)

Confessions of a Pod Person (Collection, MirrorDanse Editions 2005)

Conversations With My Cat (Co-authored with MacReady McKenzie and Ripley McKenzie, Daft Notions 2023)

The Dark Man, By Referral and Less Pleasant Tales (Collection, Daft Notions, 2024)

All I Want For Christmas (Novella, Daft Notions, 2024)

Time Spent With A Cat (Novella, Daft Notions 2024)

Story Acknowledgements

'Daily Grind' © Chuck McKenzie. First published in *Infinitas Bookshop Newsletter*, 2004

'Time Spent With a Cat' © Chuck McKenzie. First published in *Who Sleuthed It?*, Clan Destine Press, 2021. Ed. Lindy Cameron.

'Ten Tales of Astounding Science Fiction' (original title 'Ten Tales of Speculative Fiction') © Chuck McKenzie. First published in *Antipodean SF*, 2004. Ed. Ion Newcombe.

'Incident at Five-Mile Creek' © Chuck McKenzie. First published in *Agog! Fantastic Fiction*, Agog! Press, 2002. Ed. Cat Sparks.

'Marlowe Strawl' © Chuck McKenzie. First published in *Antipodean SF* Issue 91, 2006. Ed. Ion Newcombe.

'Catflap' © Chuck McKenzie. First published *Aurealis* Issue 29, 2002. Ed. Keith Stevenson.

'Full Circle' © Chuck McKenzie. First published in *Antipodean SF* Issue 66, 2003. Ed. Ion Newcombe.

'Alien Space Nazis Must Die!' © Chuck McKenzie. First published in *Elsewhere*, CSFG Publishing, 2003. Ed. Michael Barry.

'Conquest!' © Chuck McKenzie. First published in *Antipodean SF* Issue 46, 2002. Ed, Ion Newcombe.

'Tools of the Trade' © Chuck McKenzie. First published in *AustrAlien Absurdities: Comic Tales of Science-Fiction, Fantasy & Horror by Australian Authors*, Agog! Press, 2001. Ed. Chuck McKenzie & Tansy Rayner Roberts.

'Catfish' © Chuck McKenzie. Original to this collection.

'Andromeda Spaceways Pre-Booking Guide' © Chuck McKenzie. First published in *Andromeda Spaceways Inflight Magazine* Issue 1, 2002. Ed. Ben Payne.

'Old Habits Die' © Chuck McKenzie. First published in *Antipodean SF* Issue 37, 2001. Ed. Ion Newcombe.

'Customer Service' © Chuck McKenzie. First published in *Planet Relish* 2003.

'Tragedy' © Chuck McKenzie. First published in *Antipodean SF*, 2005. Ed. Ion Newcombe.

'Wiping the Smile Off' © Chuck McKenzie. First published in *Antipodean SF*, 2005.

'All I Want For Christmas' © Chuck McKenzie. First published by Daft Notions, 2024. This novella is expanded from a short story of the same title, first published in Confessions of a Pod Person', Mirrordanse Editions, 2005.

Also By

CHUCK McKENZIE

CONVERSATIONS WITH MY CAT

What does Schrödinger's Cat have to do with a chewed computer cord? How do you fit work around a cat's napping schedule? Why do cats change their minds as soon as you open the door for them?

These and other conundrums are addressed in this collection of discussions between one man and his cat, wherein are tackled many of the greatest issues of our time: politics, religion, culture, history, human rights, and poop.

You'll laugh, you'll cry, it'll change your life. Or not. Frankly, we'll say anything to get you to buy this book, which is – fair warning – NOT FOR KIDS, as the cat featured herein is a real pottymouth.

Also By

CHUCK McKENZIE
THE DARK MAN, BY REFERRAL
AND LESS PLEASANT TALES

STEP INTO THE WORLD OF THE DARK MAN:

PLEASE HAVE YOUR REFERRAL READY...

An abused child encounters the local legendary boogeyman, and finds himself querying the definition of 'monster'...

Two time-travellers observe The Crucifixion, and discover a horror far beyond the brutality of the event itself...

An inhuman predator establishes its feeding ground in a small rural town —but does it have competition...?

In this collection, representing the darker work of author Chuck McKenzie, you'll find tales of zombies, kaiju, and alien invaders; of visits to Hell, and to quiet suburban streets; of Lovecraftian entities and spectral terrors.

And other, far less pleasant tales than these...

Also By

CHUCK McKENZIE
ALL I WANT FOR CHRISTMAS

++the g'norr are
your friends —
welcome them — love,
serve, obey++

It's Christmastime, and a full-scale covert alien invasion is underway!

Bullied back into service, retired g'norr squadleader Sneet must help claim the primitive planet Earth for the glory of the G'norr Dominion by undertaking a mission that involves brainwashing human children in preparation for the takeover... all while working undercover as a shopping mall Santa.

With the might and technology of a galaxy-spanning extraterrestrial empire pitted against a bunch of primitive juvenile primates, nothing could possibly go wrong. Right?
Right...?

Also By

CHUCK McKENZIE
TIME SPENT WITH A CAT

Time Spent With A Cat: the best Hard SF gonzo-fantasy murder-mystery novella featuring a possibly-imaginary talking cat you'll ever read, probably.

My name's Jim Carpenter. I'm a private eye.
And business has been in the toilet since everyone found themselves saddled with an ethereal entity that floats beside them. Mine is a wiseass talking cat. I hate cats.
But's that's not my biggest problem, because a cashed-up frenemy from my military days has just given me six hours to solve the murder of a scientist who was working on something very special for the Special Weapons Division. Shot in the head, only one possible killer, witnesses on the scene within seconds.

Should be an easy case, right?

Except that, impossibly, the weapon and bullet have both vanished.

And the clock is ticking.

Publisher of the Niche,
the Oddball,
the Unsettling…

Small press publisher operating out of Melbourne, Australia.

Current and forthcoming publications include science fiction and horror titles, management guides, single-author collections, novels and novellas, and funny cat books.

For more information and to purchase our titles go to:
www.daftnotions.com